Factory 309:
The Trouble with Drones

by R. L. Valentine

Violet Hill Press

Factory 309:
The Trouble with Drones
by R. L. Valentine

Published by Violet Hill Press
First Paperback Edition
November 2015

ISBN 13: 978-0692579152
ISBN 10: 069257915X

For our parents and our entire family

With love and appreciation

Chapter 1

RUN! GET OUT OF HERE! SECURITY IS ON TO US! THEY'RE CLOSING THE TUNNEL DOORS!

***

MEMO:
To: Mr. Charles Milton, CEO
From: Security, AWDCOR Factory 309
Re: Infiltrators

Mr. Milton,

We're pleased to report that an infiltration attempt by several persons posing as robotic technicians has been thwarted. The actual robotic subcontractors weren't scheduled to begin until next week. We're not sure who sent them, but that doesn't matter now. The tunnel took care of everything.

Regards,
Factory 309 Security

To: Norbert Goff
From: Charles Milton
Re: Factory Security

Norb, there's been a security breach at Factory 309. Send in your undercover team to investigate. Find out if we have a problem. TOP PRIORITY. LEVEL 6.

Charles Milton, CEO, Advanced Weapons Development Corporation (AWDCOR)

***

"It'll be good to get home to the wife and kids tonight," Jake Worthington said, as he sat with his feet propped up on his desk, dipping a chocolate donut into his afternoon cup of coffee.

Before his partner, Ed Shaw, could answer, an incoming message chimed in both their ear-coms. It was sent anonymously and shouldn't have been allowed through the company's mail server. After they received it, the message deleted itself. That shouldn't have happened either.

Ed frowned at Jake as he grasped the meaning of the message:

"You *w-will* file a favorable report on Factory 309 or your families *w-will* suffer."

Jake activated his Brain Implant and saved the message while it was fresh in his mind. Ed couldn't store it. Unlike Jake, he had never held a government enforcer job and didn't have an implant.

Ed and Jake weren't just partners—they were good friends as well. Each had saved the other's life on more than one occasion. The company they worked for, AWDCOR, was in the advanced weapons development and tactical communication business. Their job was to investigate employee misconduct involving company secrets and theft. Their latest assignment had been given to them yesterday, but their boss was dragging his feet and hadn't given them the green light yet. They would be investigating a possible security breach at Factory 309, one of the company's high-technology weapons factories on Barros. The off-planet site produced various types of weapons for government and corporate uses.

"Wasn't that strange, Ed? The voice in the message was monotone, so there was no way to voice print it. It deleted itself after we heard it. But why all the freaking fuss over this particular investigation? Threatening our families over a security breach on a remote planet? It's not like we're tracking down an AWDCOR employee selling weapons to known criminals. Our transport isn't ready yet, and we still haven't decided on our cover story. I don't like it," Jake said, putting down his half-eaten donut.

"Maybe somebody's playing a joke on us. We didn't make a lot of friends when we busted the financial department for giving out unauthorized bonus checks to their friends."

Ed wondered if he should report this message to their boss. Norbert Goff wasn't the best boss around, but he stayed out of their hair most of the time. Ed knew Jake wouldn't talk to Norb about this message. The two weren't on the best of terms since an unfortunate incident that took place a month ago when Jake accidentally shot the CEO of the company, Mr. Milton. Jake was lucky that Ed had recently insisted upon changing their standard PW-2 weapons to the latest DNA-seeking PW-10, which AWDCOR had begun to manufacture. Jake had never been a good shot. He had tried his best to shoot the assassins that were dressed as food chefs, but he had hit Mr. Milton and a bodyguard instead. Fortunately, the smart projectiles had worked as designed: As soon as they penetrated the flesh of Mr. Milton and his bodyguard, they recognized known DNA within the company's database and released knock-out sedatives instead of activating their lethal mode. Ed's own projectiles had hit their intended targets and had worked like a charm. As soon as they slammed into the body armor of the assassins, they released a fast-acting acid designed to dissolve any dense substance. A second charge inside the projectiles kicked them through. The DNA sensors worked in less than 1/20 of a second, selecting the "kill" mode and releasing their lethal toxins before the assassins could carry out their mayhem. These smart "bullets" were expensive and difficult to manufacture, but they were well justified.

The local police, as usual, had merely noted the situation and had immediately released the bodies of the assassins to AWDCOR's funeral department for cremation. After all, the incident had only involved AWDCOR and had been quickly resolved. Although he hadn't been fired over the incident, Norb had been thoroughly chewed out by the CEO. Norb, in turn, had quickly demoted Jake to a junior partner position beneath Ed. Of course, Ed still treated Jake as his senior. Ed knew all about weapons and stuff, but Jake was the real brains. Ed was merely the enforcer.

Jake was already talking to his wife on his desk screen as he put an extra PW-10 ammo clip in his pocket.

"Honey—round up the kids and the dog. Don't open the door to anyone until I get home."

"Oh, no, not another one of *those* problems."

"Yeah—I know—it's upsetting—but this isn't the first time I've put you on red alert. You know the routine. I'll be home in a few minutes. It's probably nothing more than a disgruntled AWDCOR worker playing a joke."

"Heads up, Ed," Jake said, suddenly firing his PW-10 at a target on the other side of the room. It made a muffled pop as another pockmark appeared on the perimeter of the target, missing the bull's eye completely.

Ed shook his head. "Jake, I'm telling you this as a friend. You may be good-looking. You may be fit and trim. Becky and your kids may think the world of you, but you really need to target practice more—even if Norb gets upset that each shot costs 500 credits."

Jake nodded in agreement, holstered his PW-10, and gulped the last of his coffee. "Later—" he said, waving to Ed. "We'll figure this out tomorrow. I hate it when we have to work on weekends."

***

Ed and his father went out for their usual walk around the block after dinner. His father was semi-retired and supervised weapon maintenance at AWDCOR. Since they both had indoor jobs, they enjoyed these times together in the fresh air.

When they saw their favorite bench on the walking trail near the community pond was vacant, they sat down to enjoy the view. It promised to be a perfect evening. The air was calm and cool. The sun was just beginning to set on the horizon, painting the sky with dramatic streaks of purple and orange. They were in the middle of the city, but there were enough trees, hedges, and specialized fences around their neighborhood to muffle the sound of the traffic in the distance.

"You know what this reminds me of, Ed?" his

father asked, settling comfortably onto the bench. "This reminds me of that last summer when you and your mom and I went camping at the lake. Do you remember? We'd go for long walks during the day and sit on the dock at sunset, watching the open sky and water, just waiting for another fish to jump onto our hooks. . . . Sometimes you don't know how good you have it until it's gone. . . . Your mom got sick soon after that. By the time the winter holidays came, she was gone. But I'll always remember that last summer. It was the best. It was the best time of my life, actually. I didn't know it then, but it was. And it was all because of Mom—and you. That's what this reminds me of. Do you remember?"

Ed glanced at his father and then looked away. Maybe it was the dimming light, but his father looked a little pale this evening. "Yep, Dad. I remember. That was the best summer ever."

They sat in silence for several minutes, watching the sun descend on the horizon, remembering that last summer at the lake without saying anything else aloud. Yes, that was the best summer ever. When Ed stretched out his legs and closed his eyes, it almost felt like they were there again.

After another minute of peaceful silence, he opened his eyes and noticed a slight blur in the sky directly ahead of them. At first he thought it might be a small flock of water fowl winging its way toward the pond. But a moment later, the blur shifted. He could see the outline of a door or a hatch in the middle of it.

How strange, Ed thought, sitting up straighter on the bench, turning to point it out to his father.

A second later, as he was still thinking about that last summer when Mom was still alive, he felt his skin beginning to burn. He leaned toward his father as quickly as he could, but he didn't have time to push him aside or even to take another breath.

It was already too late for that. Much too late.

Chapter 2

Jake slept that night, but not as soundly as he usually did. He got up several times to check on the security system and to look in on Lucy and Jacob, just to be sure they were all right. They were both sound asleep in their bedrooms, oblivious to any problems. Fluffy, their guard dog, was sleeping in the middle of the hall and didn't budge when Jake stepped over him.

At dawn, when the twin moons were beginning to fade on the horizon, Jake's boss called. That wasn't good. Norb never called him at home.

Becky turned in her sleep and moaned. The bedside com screen indicated Norb was using the company's code red alert. The situation must be very serious.

"Jake—are you okay?" Norb's face was drawn, and his voice sounded different. He wasn't using his usual boss-to-employee tone. Jake noted he was at work, which was rather early for him.

"We're all fine here," Jake answered. "What's up?"

Norbert started mumbling something, but Jake

didn't catch his meaning.

Norb tried again. "They just burned up! There's nothing left but a couple of piles of ashes!"

"What burned up?"

Norb hesitated for only a moment."Ed!" he blurted out "—and his father!"

Jake broke the connection, jumped out of bed, and grabbed his PW-10, which was propped against the wall near the bed. *To hell with Norb. I've got to protect my family.*

"What's going on?" Becky asked, still half asleep.

"We've got to get you and the kids to a safe location."

"What?"

Jake was already dressed when Becky scrambled out of bed and ran down the hall to wake up the kids. He could hear Fluffy barking and the kids complaining about the early hour as he considered his options. Actually, maybe Norb could help. He had resources available for this type of thing. Besides being his immediate supervisor, Norb was in charge of several Advanced Weapons factories, including Factory 309 on Barros. He knew a lot of people and had a lot of connections.

When Jake called Norb back and asked for help in hiding his family, he agreed and was actually nice about it. He didn't even hint at getting something in return. After they spoke, Jake called for a company armored vehicle and was pleased to find out that Norb had already dispatched one to their address.

The armored vehicle took them to the company's executive drop-off. Norb was waiting on the curb and seemed a little nervous. When Jake started helping the kids out of their seats, Norb yelled to the driver and the guard to let Jake out and take his family to site H, which was company code for a hideaway location. Jake hugged everyone goodbye and told them everything would be okay in just a short time. After he hugged Becky again, he patted Fluffy on the head and exited from the van's rear door.

Norb motioned to Jake. "Follow me."

Jake glanced back as the armored van drove away with his family and then silently followed his boss.

They went to Norb's office, which was one floor beneath the CEO's office. Jake remained standing while Norb sat down and checked his status/alert/mail screens. Jake was still thinking about his family and Ed when Norb finally acknowledged him by pointing to a chair.

"Your family should be safe by now. . . . The way Ed and his father were killed can't happen. I mean, they were just sitting there and whoosh— blue flames, smoke, fire. The bench was burned in half. Nobody saw anything before it happened. No robot assassins or laser beam traces. Nothing. No signs of explosives or chemical agents either. Jake, you're lucky this didn't happen to you or your family." Norb was obviously upset, but Jake had the feeling he was concerned about something that had nothing to do with Ed or his father.

Jake and Ed always had enemies looking for payback, but nobody had ever gotten close before. Ed often joked about the dozens of drone bombs he received that were camouflaged as legitimate packages. The drone reception pad at his home, like Jake's, was equipped with ultra-sensitive explosive and biochemical detectors and disposal systems. The bombing attempts always ended rather noisily. Sometimes the drone pad had to repaired, but no one had ever been hurt before.

After Jake reviewed his assignment on Barros,

Norb dismissed him with a wave of his hand. Nothing about the assignment seemed unusual. It shouldn't take too long. He just needed to investigate a possible security breach at Factory 309. It surprised him when Norb said the assignment would be scrubbed if it were up to him, but the CEO was pushing it. Norb also mumbled something about a replacement partner, but Jake was still thinking about his family and Ed and didn't hear exactly what he said.

Hell of a time to be going off planet, Jake thought, as he gathered his usual spaceflight trip kit from his office and ordered a taxi-bot.

When he closed his office door behind him, he tried not to look back at Ed's empty desk. He needed to stay focused. The sooner he left, the sooner he would be back home with his family.

Chapter 3

At the Welton spaceport entrance door, Jake paused and glanced in the direction of his house, wondering where Becky and the kids were right now.

"Going in or *not?*" the irritated automatic voice at the door inquired.

"In," Jake answered, punching in the code without looking back again. He needed to concentrate on the job ahead.

After he inserted his hand into the DNA detector at the guard station, he was allowed to bypass the scan station, since he was authorized to carry a weapon. He proceeded to the AWDCOR terminal without any further delay.

He had already alerted the company's space travel department to prep his favorite ship. They had been somewhat evasive when he spoke to them about it. He had ordered the ship to be upgraded with the latest crypsis camouflage system a month ago. Spaceships were less likely to be fired upon if you couldn't see them. He had also requested that the ship revert to snazzy flame-shaped racing stripes whenever the camo was inactive. He hoped everything was completed and ready for this flight. His ship was a 4-passenger scout with extensive stealth capability. It had limited weapons, relying on its camo and speed to avoid head-on fights.

Jake started getting anxious when he couldn't see his ship in its regular berth. His ear-com chimed. Another surprise call from Norb was coming in.

"Your ship is on line and fully functional with the new camouflage system. Get going. It's over at Berth 3. Your new partner is already on board."

Jake was relieved his boss was actually doing something right for a change.

The ship's new camo looked great—that is— you could hardly see it at all until you almost walked into it. His new partner must have already activated the preliminary countdown to test the camo. Jake was glad he wasn't wasting any time. The crypsis camouflage wasn't usually activated in the spaceport in order to avoid mishaps.

As he was taking the open elevator up to the entry hatch, Jake kept noticing a strange chemical smell. The new paint must not be fully cured. Just before he reached the entry hatch, the camo system switched offline, revealing the ship's stylish red and yellow racing stripes. He had to admit he was very pleased with them. They made him feel young again.

Through the open hatch, he could see that a rather young-looking person was already in the co-pilot's chair watching the countdown status screen. *It figures they sent me a newbie.*

The newbie jerked around and looked at Jake as if he had never seen a middle-aged bald guy before. "I'm Tom Calwell—your partner for this assignment."

Jake was fairly certain Tom was a company-raised orphan, a GAP. Gene Altered Persons were genetically modified to fit the company's parameters. Jake was glad he was a GAP. They weren't known to disobey commands or hold back in a firefight.

After they finished the final take-off check list, the ship was rolled to the vertical launcher and latched into place. The skyscraper-sized launcher, which saved fuel they might need later, would accelerate the ship to 5 Gs.

"You're cleared for launch, AWDCOR Scout

45," the ship's com screen announced.

Jake looked at the status screens one more time and then touched the com screen.

"Port control, AWDCOR Scout 45 is now launching. . . ." Jake took a deep breath. "Well, here we go—" he said to Tom, toggling the launch switch.

The force of the launch slammed them back into their flight chairs and propelled them into space in less than 5 minutes. The ship's navi-screen indicated everything was okay to proceed to Barros. They switched off their engines and switched on the camo, which would make the ship very difficult to detect. Barros was 7 hours away. It was a small desert-like planet, a good place to manufacture weapons and munitions. AWDCOR and other companies had several manufacturing sites there.

"Take over, Tom. Put it on autopilot. I'm going to rest a bit and think about what we need to do when we land."

Chapter 4

The trip was uneventful, except when another civilian ship and its well-armed escort were detected close by. Owners of civilian spaceships usually couldn't afford camo systems and had to hire armed escorts for protection. With the camouflage active on Jake's scout, other ships went by without ever knowing of their presence.

As they got close to Barros, the navi-computer made contact and set up a landing schedule. No voice contact was made because this was a corporate business ship on a prearranged assignment. The camo would normally be switched off during landing to avoid mishaps with other aircraft. For some reason, it hadn't completely switched off this time. Jake didn't like technical glitches, but this could be handled. He told Tom to switch on the laser landing blinkers, making sure they were at maximum brightness and repetition. That would make them more visible as they landed.

The navi-screen announced atmosphere entry

was about to begin. In spite of his efforts to concentrate on his mission, Jake couldn't stop himself from thinking about his family and how he should be back home looking after them. He snapped to full alert when the audio warnings sounded, and Tom started yelling something about the ship being on fire. The ship's status screens were flashing red. The hull temperature was climbing way beyond normal.

"What the hell's going on?" Jake shouted.

"I don't know!" Tom yelled back.

The hull temperature had reached a critical point. The ship's control systems were in jeopardy. They had only a few seconds before their ship would turn into a fiery ball and crash into the spaceport. Tom's GAP indoctrination kicked in. Without a word of warning, he activated Jake's ejection seat system but not his own.

The force of Jake's exit from the ship felt like another launch into space. When his parachute opened and he began to drift toward the ground, he watched the burning scout as it continued its wild, erratic descent. He knew what Tom was attempting to do. He was trying to manipulate any control that would guide the ship to an uninhabited area. It was no use. Jake watched helplessly as it crashed and exploded in a nearby parking lot. Several vehicles were destroyed on impact. Others were quickly engulfed in flames. Jake thought he heard screams coming from one of the burning vehicles.

Had Tom somehow survived? It didn't look good. Tom was only a GAP, but the guy had been nice enough—and he had just saved his life. GAPs were both envied and despised. They received free vocational training and free medical services, as well as a guarantee of lifetime employment with their parent company. Genetic modifications fixed any serious gene mutations, helping them to look young during their long lifespan. Poor Tom. Being a Genetically Altered Person hadn't worked out well for him at all.

Jake's ejection device was about to touch down near the spaceport. Much to his relief, a group of the local police was already gathering on the ground below him. They should help him figure out this blazing mess. Strange, though. They seemed to be assembling in a tactical formation around his landing spot. A moment later, they drew their weapons in unison and aimed them directly at him.

What the hell?

Chapter 5

"Don't even think about making a move of any kind!" the tactical chief yelled.

Jake could see they were deadly serious. Their PW-2 weapons, which were still aimed directly at him, were blinking red, meaning they were set to kill-on-contact. That usually only happened in an all-out firefight or when taking down a known criminal. Jake sighed and froze in place.

As soon as he touched down, three guards grabbed him at once, one on each arm, while the other unhooked his ejection harness straps. They cuffed his arms and legs, snapped a lethal shock collar around his neck, searched him with a portable full-body scanner, and then hand-patted him from head to toe. He knew his Brain Implant would be shielded from the scan. It would just show up as a tiny tumor. They took his ear-com, along with his PW-10. His hygiene unit was left in place, but all his pocket items were removed.

Without saying a word, they slammed him into a prisoner transfer chair and attached its restraints to his arms and legs. The chair looked like a superstrong wheelchair without hand wheels and was remote-controlled by the guards.

Jake knew how things worked with these local police units. It was best to remain passive and not ask any questions—or even talk at all. There was always one guard who wanted to see somebody twitch—or even die—via the shock collar. He kept his mouth shut as they rolled him into the back of the paddy wagon.

A dark memory came to Jake during the ride to police headquarters. He had experienced a catastrophic crash once before, during his time with the government's Readiness and Support Department. He was piloting an incursion ship with several troopers on board. The target had been a small warehouse where the control center for a space pirate was located. He was hung over at the time, still feeling the effects of a wild weekend party, which included too much drinking and an intense virtual reality episode. Somehow, he switched off the autopilot during the ship's descent and allowed the ship to go into freefall. His reactions had been slow and confused. He made it worse by trying to turn the ship and accelerating back into orbit. The ship was going down too fast for its steering jets to work—its hull was already melting. The troopers survived, but the ship was a complete loss. Jake was demoted and eventually released from government service. His record included medals for valor, so the event was merely listed as pilot error, and he soon found a new job with AWDCOR. The company needed his skill set and didn't really care about anything else in his past. Jake had matured after that and had settled down with Becky.

The police van suddenly stopped, jolting Jake back to reality. He had suppressed that memory for nearly two decades. His prisoner transport chair was guided down the van's ramp and into the police station's back entrance.

The police captain was young, way too young for his position. He had to be a GAP.

"You're under arrest for the murder of Thomas Calwell, an employee of the Advanced Weapons Development Corporation, willful destruction of an AWDCOR scout ship, and the murders of three parking lot attendants. Your superior has been duly notified of your execution." The police boss's tone was flat. "Do you wish to make a statement for archival purposes?"

Jake knew better than to say too much. His

past government record with the RS Department would no doubt be recanted and used against him. His next few words would probably be his last.

"I'm on a Code 6 AWDCOR assignment. If Thomas Calwell were here, he would verify that our ship was somehow sabotaged. . . . Tell my family I love them."

After Jake spoke, he looked straight ahead, knowing his execution would probably be the next order of business. Since he was a company employee, the method would be quick with no news coverage. He wondered how his family would be able to survive. This type of employee death wouldn't be covered by the company insurance plan.

The police captain motioned to someone who was standing near the door. A moment later, Jake was on his way to a holding cell, still restrained in the mobile prisoner chair. So far, so good. Executions were usually immediate. When the cell door slammed shut, he kept thinking about his family, wishing he could see them one more time.

The wall screen in his cell came alive. The police superintendent, an older lady, appeared on the screen and announced his execution was on hold for a few minutes. It was obvious to Jake that they were communicating with his boss and/or the CEO of AWDCOR about his situation.

An eternity seemed to pass before the screen came on again, and the superintendent announced there would be a further delay with his pending execution. Jake sighed and began to consider recent events in an investigative mode, quickly reviewing everything in his mind from the time he and Ed had received the anonymous message about Factory 309.

Who killed Ed and his father? How were they reduced to a pile of ashes without any trace of a weapon? Why was Norb so uncharacteristically concerned, offering to help my family? Why did our ship burn up on a routine descent, conveniently leaving nothing behind to investigate? None of it made any sense, but everything must be connected to Factory 309.

Jake yawned. He had been awake for much too long. He wished he could lie down, but he could do nothing but tilt his head back slightly in the prisoner chair and succumb to physical exhaustion.

Chapter 6

Jake woke up to the sound of his boss talking through the com screen in his jail cell.

"Jake Worthington, I see you're sitting in the messy end of the latrine," Norb was saying. "You know, if this assignment hadn't been raised by Mr. Milton to Level 10 now, I could have been too busy to respond to the Barros police advisory."

Norb's tone of voice and facial expression had assumed their usual master-to-servant mode. Jake was still waking up, longing for some breakfast and coffee, when Norb's message hit home. They weren't going to execute him and would probably even release him so he could continue his assignment.

"One other item, FYI," Norb continued, "the contractors who installed your new camouflage system admitted they may have used an untested crypsis generator. You insisted on having fancy racing stripes when the camo was inactive. The incompatibility between your stripes and their crypsis generator may have caused the fire. . . .

Anyway, their admission was enough to spring you from jail, in spite of your past record with the government."

Jake's preference for a ship with a little style and pizzazz had been a deadly mistake. "How's my family—can I talk to them?"

"Let's review your assignment first."

As usual, Norb's top priority was company business. Jake listened as Norb went on, outlining the details of his assignment on Barros—to investigate Factory 309. Jake wondered if it was smart to discuss everything so openly. This com screen was in a police cell. It was supposed to be a secure connection, but he knew how easy it was to circumvent such connections.

"Look, just send any updates to my ear-com later, and I'll go from there," Jake told Norb. He hoped his ear-com hadn't been compromised while in police hands.

"Okay," Norb answered. He broke the connection without giving Jake any information about his family.

***

Later that morning, three guards came into Jake's cell. Two of them kept joking between themselves that they might go ahead and kill him anyway. They were still smirking and laughing as the third guard released him from his prisoner chair and un-cuffed him. Jake didn't say anything. He just stretched his legs and rubbed his wrists, relieved to be on his feet again.

As he was being led to a public shower and dressing area, something strange happened. His Brain Implant flashed an alert to his mind. Another person with a government-issued BI had been detected in the area. The operational distance for a BI was limited to less than 30 steps, unless someone had an enhanced BI. But enhanced BIs were rare, since their large size eventually caused brain damage. A government agent was undoubtedly somewhere nearby. BIs were only given to a few select government agents because of the expense and inherent problems involved. Brain surgery was always risky, especially when a device was hooked into cognitive areas of the mind.

After Jake's BI alerted him that another BI was within the area, a guard standing near the door must have noticed his expression.

"Are you all right?" he asked.

Jake shrugged. "I was just thinking about my

family and going home," he answered, as he handed his clothes to the mobile washer/dryer. The guard nodded and didn't say anything else.

When Jake sat down at a public com screen in the police station, he felt much better. A quick shower and a clean set of clothes had made him feel almost like a person again. Within a few minutes, the connection to AWDCOR was granted, and Norb's data file was downloaded to his ear-com. The assignment was still the same, except it was now at a Level 10, which allowed him more leeway with covert actions.

While he was sitting at the com screen, he knew he was being watched. He pretended to be waiting for another message while he switched his BI from STANDBY to ON. Now he could send thoughts directly from his mind, and any other BI-equipped person in the area would be able to detect his BI. As soon as he set his BI to ON, someone immediately flashed a short message to his mind.

I am a RS government agent and need assistance. Who are you?

Jake wondered why there were no other government agents within the signal range of this agent's implant to help. The whole idea of an implanted com unit was to coordinate with a partner or team. It took Jake a while to formulate his answer and send it. He often used his BI to store messages, but he hadn't tried to send thoughts for a long time.

Yeah, he answered, *I'm an ex-government RS agent. What's your situation?*

The agent replied quickly. *I'm so glad you're here! The local police locked me up for being in the vicinity of a GAP training academy near Factory 309. They won't let me talk to anybody. I doubt if they've even told anyone in my department that I'm being held.*

Jake frowned. This government agent must be investigating Factory 309. But why would the government back home on Dormir be concerned about an internal corporate problem? If there had been a security breach at Factory 309, it was probably related to corporate spying. And almost all corporate spying involved other corporate agents looking for secret designs. The government RS group only became involved when a CEO or employee went rogue. The government people dealt with those situations directly, without any regard to normal civilian policies. Jake would have to be very careful dealing with this RS agent. His simple assignment was turning out to be more complicated than he originally thought.

The RS Bureau was a Readiness and Support group that was supposed to help other government agencies and ensure they were ready to perform their allocated functions. But everyone knew its real role was to enforce corporate government mandates. These mandates had been around for a long time and seemed to resolve the ever-present conflicts between government, corporate, and civilian needs. The RS Department kept the corporate entities from total anarchy, while still allowing them the freedom to conduct their business without any serious oversight. If they harmed innocents or non-corporate civilians too much, the government would react via the civilian authorities or sometimes with special government enforcement units. It was truly a dog-eat-dog setup, but it seemed to work. Everyone had jobs, and the corporations paid for their infrastructure, which included roads, spaceships, housing, schools, hospitals, etc.. The bigger corporations owned whole planets or moons and ran things pretty much as they saw fit.

He decided he couldn't help the RS agent now. The poor chap would have to stay in jail. But Jake would try to alert the RS Department back home about the situation. That would give him time to finish his own assignment and still satisfy his obligation to his former employer. He owed them something. After all, they could have locked him away for the incident in his early days.

RS agent, I'll try to alert your department about your predicament, Jake messaged through his Brain Implant, as he got up from the com screen and retrieved his ear-com and pocket items from the police booth. Frankly, he didn't want to hear any more from this agent. This was one of those times that he regretted not taking the risk of having his BI removed when he left government service. The odds of successful removal were only one in four. Three out of four times a person could be left in a permanent comatose state—or worse.

It was almost noon when Jake exited the police station. As he paused for a moment to take a breath of fresh air and to shield his eyes from the intensity of the sun, he set his BI to STANDBY mode by selecting the proper code in his mind. He could have switched it to OFF, but it might be smarter to know if other BIs were being used in his proximity.

Chapter 7

The taxi-bot Jake had ordered was already waiting for him in front of the police station. The jail cell had unsettled him. He needed to get out into the open air. After the taxi-bot validated his DNA imprint and charged the standard basic fee to his account, he programmed it to take him to a local park.

The park was a typical company layout. It included several walking trails, a few rides for the kids, and family-sized pagodas with facilities. The walking trails meandered through the dry terrain, past several automatic drinking fountains and cactus gardens that were in full bloom. It was good to be out of jail—and out of the horrible confinement of the prisoner chair. He didn't even mind the heat of the noonday sun. That actually made the park even more pleasant for him, since most people had abandoned it for the hottest part of the day.

After he had stretched his legs for a while, Jake sat down on a stone bench near a small pond with a fountain. He was still shaken by Ed's death and the catastrophic loss of his ship and his new partner. It was hard to concentrate on his assignment. He needed to find out what kind of security breach had taken place at Factory 309. Had the design for a new secret weapon been compromised? Was someone trying to sell top-secret information?

As he was watching a scorpion with two stingers seeking the shade of a nearby cactus, a shadow from behind him made him reach instinctively for his PW-10. But he had forgotten that the police had kept it. He realized the person behind him had the advantage, and it was already too late to do anything, but Jake turned his head anyway to see his would-be assassin. He and Ed had encountered several people on Barros who might be looking for payback. He wanted to see exactly who it was.

He found himself staring into the business end of an illegal large-diameter pellet blaster. That was bad enough, but the person on the other end of it seemed very familiar.

"Tom Calwell was my brother and best friend," the young man said, pointing his weapon a little closer. "I can't let his murderer just walk out of jail without paying for his crime. Do you have any last words? Oh—by the way—my name is Ryan Calwell. I want you to know exactly who it is that's gonna kill you."

Jake realized Ryan was a GAP with the same appearance, genetics, and upbringing as Tom Calwell. He was surprised that Ryan's indoctrination and training hadn't stopped him from threatening an unarmed company employee. This guy was bent on revenge. He would need to choose his words carefully.

"First of all, I didn't kill Tom Calwell. The ship was on fire. He ejected my flight chair before I could stop him. He saved my life. I owe him a life-debt."

Jake's words didn't seem to matter at all. Ryan merely smiled slightly and raised his weapon a little higher, obviously enjoying the moment. In the next few seconds, this guy was going to blow his head off. So much for the GAP obedience training regime.

Ryan's finger was beginning to twitch on the trigger when another man suddenly emerged from behind a cactus.

"Ryan, his story sort of checks out. My source says this guy is a company detective. Tom's crash is being listed as an accident, but if you want to shoot him, go ahead. It won't bother me. He's one of those AWDCOR executive types."

Jake suppressed a sigh as Ryan frowned and then slipped his short-barreled weapon under his shirt.

"Look, Baldy," Ryan said, "we know you're here to investigate something. You have to help us with a problem—or next time I won't give you time to do any fancy talking."

"All right—I understand your terms. What's your problem?"

Ryan straddled the other end of the bench and sat down facing him, while the man near the cactus stood by as a lookout. These guys were obviously on the run from somebody.

"It's kind of complicated. We sort of killed our supervisor," Ryan said.

"He had it coming," the lookout said, glancing from side to side, watching the immediate area.

"Anyway," Ryan continued, "the company was testing a new weapon. Our supervisor decided to play weapons-test engineer when the members of the technical crew were on their lunch break. They left the weapon's control station switched on.

Several GAP children died as a result. They burned up in a cloud of blue smoke. Nothing was left of them but little piles of ashes. Our stupid supervisor was going to place the blame on us—the GAPs. The company would have believed him—we would have been executed. " Ryan paused as the scorpion with the double stinger walked over the toe of his boot and then continued on its way. Jake expected Ryan to stand up and flatten it, but he didn't. He merely kicked a little dust onto its stingers and watched it scurry away.

"So," Ryan went on, "our supervisor had a little accident involving a mixing vat and molten steel. We would have been okay—nothing was left of him at all—but a vat camera recorded everything. Security didn't believe us when we said he accidentally fell into the vat, especially when a certain picture showed four people tossing him in."

"If I had been there," Jake said, "I would have helped you toss him in. My senior partner and his father were killed in a similar manner a few days ago. . . . I'll try to help you—but you may need to assist me later. I'll meet you here tomorrow."

Ryan looked irritated after he said that. Jake hoped he wasn't going to open his shirt and show him his weapon again.

When he and his lookout remained silent, Jake got up from the bench and walked away from the two men without glancing back at them. As he was leaving the area, he noticed two more guys hanging around, watching him.

Jake decided to take a walking trail to the AWDCOR guest hotel. He needed to think, and the walk would be welcomed exercise, even during the hottest part of the day on Barros.

Chapter 8

As he was heading back to the hotel, Jake realized his assignment had changed from a security breach investigation to the misuse of a secret weapon. The weapon had all the earmarks of being something that was illegal. AWDCOR could be in a lot of trouble. He needed to act quickly. He decided he would pose as a company safety inspector. It wasn't too far off from his actual job classification anyway.

The AWDCOR hotel was in the middle of town. It catered mostly to AWDCOR customers and executives.

"Good evening, sir," a robot announced as he was entering the main entrance. "Welcome to our Hotel. The check-in lobby is to your left."

A receptionist at the front desk asked Jake to place his hand in a DNA test unit. It blinked green and then automatically checked him in. After he picked up a sandwich and a drink from the lobby's buffet, he hurried to the corridor where his room was located. The door opened when his DNA imprint on the knob was verified.

With his sandwich in one hand, he immediately contacted Norb on the com screen to arrange the details necessary to complete his assignment. Of course, when he spoke to Norb, Jake didn't mention anything about his intention to get Ryan and his co-workers off the hook. He could investigate their supervisor's "accident" while he was snooping around about this new weapon. He hoped Ryan and his buddies would lay low. If they got captured now, Jake wouldn't be able to do much to help.

Once again, Norb ignored his request to talk to Becky and the kids. "They're doing fine," was his only response before he ended their conversation.

Jake kicked off his boots and sat down on the edge of the bed. He needed to get some rest. Tomorrow was going to be a long day.

***

Jake got up early and gulped down a quick breakfast in the lobby. A taxi-bot was already waiting for him at the hotel's entrance.

"Factory 309," Jake told the taxi. "And make it quick."

"Sir, I'm sorry," the taxi voice answered, "but that's a restricted site. I'll need authorization from AWDCOR headquarters to take you there."

"Contact Norbert Goff's office at AWDCOR on Dormir," Jake said, trying not to sound irritated. "He can give you authorization."

Amazingly, it took only a few minutes before the taxi completed the task and started on its way. Norb's computerized aide had probably handled the problem.

It promised to be another hot day on Barros. The traffic was light, and there wasn't a cloud or spaceship in the sky. The rolling, barren landscape, with groups of cactus growing in clusters, whizzed by Jake's window. The taxi was definitely fulfilling his request to make it a quick trip.

As they were nearing Factory 309, he noticed the GAP training academy. It had the usual playground and barracks. No kids were playing outside. That was odd. Morning recesses on a hot planet like Barros usually took place outdoors when the kids could enjoy the cooler part of the day.

Down the road Jake could see a flashing warning sign: RESTRICTED AREA OFFICIAL BUSINESS ONLY. He was almost there. Multiple road spikes were sticking up through the pavement but retracted just as the taxi reached them. The vehicle slowed to a stop at the first guard shack. A heavy laser weapon was aimed directly at the taxi.

"STOP NOW!" a speaker screamed. "EXIT with your hands UP and do NOT move."

Jake did as he was told and stood completely still as a beam from a remote-controlled body scanner hummed up and down his body. It was set to a high intensity. When it had completed its scan, two armed men emerged from the guard shack. One kept a PW-2 hand weapon pointed at Jake, while the other checked his DNA and fed it into the company's data base. It should have taken only a few seconds to verify he was an AWDCOR employee, but it seemed a little longer.

"Okay," the guard finally said, "you can pass after you empty your pockets and put everything in the bin. Your ear-com too. Your taxi-bot can't stay here. Tell it to leave."

The other guard, who still had his PW-2 pointed in Jake's direction, motioned him toward the gate as it opened. "Start walking," he ordered. "I'll be behind you all the way." His PW-2 was set to lethal.

A short distance ahead, Jake could see an above-ground tunnel with heavy steel flip-down doors on each side. The security here was definitely more intense than the average facility. This type of factory usually just had a 100 KV electric grid above and below ground level in a deep trench around its perimeter. The 100 KV grid electrocuted—and quickly cremated—any trespassers. AWDCOR always liked to keep everything nice and tidy.

When they approached the tunnel, Jake was sure it was mined on both sides. The desert landscape around the tunnel wasn't well maintained, unlike other areas around the factory. As they were passing through the main part of the dimly lit tunnel, his trained eye detected gas ports on each side. You wouldn't want to be trapped in here. The gas that those ports delivered was probably flammable—not your usual knock-out stuff. He glanced upward. The tunnel's walls and ceiling were covered with soot.

It took over a minute to get through the tunnel. As they were clearing it and approaching another guard shack, Jake noticed that several other laser weapons were tracking them. The guard following him stayed behind as two new guards came out and went through the same routine as before, doing another DNA test and body scan. It didn't take as long this time, but Jake noticed they kept looking at his picture displayed on their wrist com screens and pointing to him.

"Your itinerary and identity check out," one guard said, "but your picture matches a recent park entrance image. Why were you at the park?" This older guard spoke carefully and seemed to be more than a guard. He was acting like a veteran investigator. Jake was fully expecting the next image to show his encounter with Ryan. He would be in big trouble if he had been seen talking to those guys. He hoped this guard didn't have access to any more pictures and wondered why he wasn't being questioned about his recent jail time. Norb had obviously been successful in blocking or deleting that.

"I needed some exercise and time to think about some stuff," Jake said. "What's the big deal about a guy taking a walk in a park?"

"Hey, Phil," the young guard near him muttered, "we have a wise guy here. Should we keep him for a while?"

Phil didn't answer. "Just put your hand into the

tagger," he ordered Jake.

Jake slipped his hand into the opening of the tag machine and watched as it quickly attached a slender silver tag to his wrist. The skin tag would allow him to have access to various areas in the factory. Skin tags were fairly good IDs. If you tried to remove it without using the proper procedure, it would release a knock-out toxin. The status on the silver tag suddenly turned green, indicating his DNA had been vetted.

Jake glanced up at a chart on the wall that illustrated AWDCOR's skin tag information. A red tag meant access to one area only with an escort. A silver tag, like the one he had been given just now, allowed access to most areas with an escort. A gold tag allowed unlimited access. The chart also showed how the micro-sized retractable hooks attached under the skin. An antiseptic and nerve block were part of the procedure. A fast-healing sticky strip would be applied after the skin tag was removed.

Jake didn't know where to start looking in the factory, but since he was supposed to be a safety inspector investigating the supervisor's untimely demise, he requested a guide.

Phil smiled slightly. "No problem. You didn't

really think you could wander around by yourself, did you? There are some dangerous areas in this factory."

"Yeah," the younger guard said, "you could just disappear in a puff of smoke."

Phil gave the smart-aleck guard a nasty look and told him he would be Jake's guide.

The younger guard frowned and mumbled something before he motioned to Jake.

"Ok, Mr. Worthington, let's get going," he said, as he turned the DNA-secured handle that opened the entry door to Factory 309.

Chapter 9

Jake had toured many automated factories in the past. Super-smart robots and factory-trained GAPs were the norm. But Factory 309 was different. As he and his guide walked along a glassed corridor, they could look down at the assembly areas on the factory floor, which were divided into sections. Unlike other factories, none of the assembly areas included any fixed or simple droid robots, and he couldn't see many GAPs at all. An ultra-sophisticated robotic system seemed to be completely in place here. Maybe this specialized system was part of AWDCOR's concern over security leaks.

"You don't want to walk anywhere down there," his guide said, pointing to the floor below them.

Each corner of every assembly area included a coiling, snake-like tentacle with multiple tools protruding at the end. Each flexible arm, his guide explained, was computer-controlled and could do the most delicate task or move a massive final assembly. The tentacles reminded Jake of metallic snakes, slithering from task to task and even rising into the air as they went about their work. They were assembling, welding, drilling, and using a variety of snap-on tools with precise, choreographed movements.

Above the factory floor, a banner had been strung between two posts declaring Factory 309 to be the *Home of the Sticky Ball Model 3*. A customer was obviously scheduled to visit, and AWDCOR was trying to close a deal.

"Sticky Ball handheld weapons aren't that new," Jake commented. "I'm surprised the company is making them here."

"But this model has a new feature. Besides having the usual liquid dye and tear gas," his guide said proudly, "our new Sticky Ball includes micro millipede-bots that are released when the ball opens. The millipedes search out a person's skin and release a knock-out toxin or a severe itching chemical through their dainty little stinging feet." The guide laughed. "Those worms can find the smallest opening, even if the victim is fully clothed."

"It's too bad we need things like that to calm people down," Jake said. "But I guess it's better than using a PW-1 on them." A PW-1's barbed toxic projectiles required surgery to remove and sometimes caused permanent eye damage.

A mobile EMP (Electro Motive Propulsion) weapon was being constructed in the next area below them. It looked like a custom built-to-spec device for civilian police departments. The guide explained that a long, linear electronic motor built inside each tube propelled the weapon's canisters, which contained knock-out agents. Lethal agents were forbidden by the government, but it was no secret that they were sometimes used anyway. The operation of this particular weapon would be almost completely silent, keeping its location hidden from unruly mobs. AWDCOR specialized in these types of custom-built weapons. It was such a profitable business that AWDCOR had built Factory 309 within walking distance of Factory 301, which was a much larger facility that manufactured most of its standard catalog weapons.

All four tentacles were in use in the assembly area of the EMP weapon. One tentacle was busy installing control modules in the weapon's transport mechanism. The other three were making final adjustments inside the tubes. The weapon would soon be ready for final testing at the firing range.

As Jake and his guide were about to move on, a worker on the factory floor below them suddenly screamed. His arm was caught in a tentacle. Jake's guide quickly said something into his com unit. Within a second, all four tentacles in that assembly area went slack. Even from this distance, Jake could see that the GAP worker's arm was bleeding profusely and was hanging only by a ligament. He started to say something to the guide but stopped. He would let him explain it first.

"That worker wasn't supposed to be in there until his supervisor gave the all-clear signal," the guide said, apparently unconcerned about the man's injury.

Other workers were running across the factory floor now, rushing in to help. A medic-bot trailed along behind them.

"I'll have to investigate this later, but we need to move on," Jake told his guide. He noted to himself that the worker's supervisor wasn't in the rescue group. Supervisors wore bright-orange safety hats, and none could be seen in the area. There seemed to be a pattern of supervisors neglecting their primary job—to keep their teams safe at all times. That was especially critical in a dangerous weapons factory like this. Jake was beginning to realize that Norb's management style was present at Factory 309. That didn't surprise him. After all, Norb was its director. The onsite factory manager must be a complete ass or really blind to the employee safety situation here.

"Can I see where your ore-mixing vats are?"

"Okay, we'll go there, but there's not much to see in that building."

Jake had expected to be taken to a hot, noxious outside structure where specialized steel was made. His previous factory visits had been to high-tech places that used polymers and pre-formed metal parts instead of steel vats. But many weapon factories utilized specialized steel for their larger weapons. It was very strong, rust-proof, and easy to fabricate.

The steel manufacturing building was spotless, and the air was clean. The raw ore-mixing vats were enclosed and remotely operated. Jake began to wonder about the story Ryan had told him about his supervisor's death. It would be difficult, if not impossible, to toss a person into a mixing vat here. The rooms in which the vats were contained were locked tight when they were in operation. Maybe they killed him somewhere else and ditched the body in an offline vat. But even that didn't make sense. The vat sensors would detect a foreign substance and wouldn't start its ore-mixing and melting program/process. Something wasn't adding up. Jake was getting weary of this whole trip and his job. He sensed his family was in more danger now, even though they were supposed to be in a secret protected location.

"Are there any other ore-mixing vats?" Jake asked the guide.

The young man hesitated. "Look, I've seen from your tag data that you're a safety inspector. Since you have a Level 4 Security Clearance, I can say, yeah, there's a smaller unenclosed vat in building C-3. But you need a special tag to see that building. Why this sudden interest in mixing vats? I've probably already said too much. Your best bet is to look around some more and then file a report. We gotta leave this building now. They have to pour out these vats. We're in the way."

"Okay. Ore-mixing areas are known to be accident prone, that's all. Just doing my job. . . . Let's go to lunch," Jake answered, wondering if this guy was even aware that a supervisor had recently been tossed into a mixing vat.

As they were eating lunch in the cafeteria, Jake kept wondering about that other mixing vat in Building C-3. The food-bots brought a choice of burgers, fish, and veggies, plus drinks. Not bad for a company-run cafeteria.

Jake's only chance to see the other building was to somehow convince his guide to take him there or to sneak off by himself and find it. His skin tag would be a problem. He'd have to think of something else. What kind of weapon was being manufactured in Building C-3? Maybe it was connected to the deaths of Ed and his father, as well as the GAP children. It wouldn't be the first time innocents were used to test a new weapon that was still in the prototype stage and not yet licensed for use.

His attempt to suggest that his guide take him to Building C-3 didn't work. He wasn't swayed by Jake's promise to put in a good word to the company's CEO.

"Listen, Worthington! Only people with gold skin-tags or C-3 personnel are allowed in that building!"

Jake backed off, but his guide had

unknowingly helped him. Maybe Ryan and his friends were authorized to go into Building C-3. Jake told his guide he had seen enough and was ready to leave to file a report.

Chapter 10

As he was leaving the factory, the guard told Jake to stick his hand into the de-tag unit. After the tag's tiny harpoon-like needles were retracted, the tag fell off and was archived. When he retracted his hand, a healing strip had already been placed over the puncture marks on his wrist that the tag had left behind. The guard handed him a bag which contained his ear-com and personal pocket items and opened the gate without saying a word.

The taxi-bot that Jake had ordered to take him back to the company's guest hotel was already waiting for him at the gate. As they passed the GAP academy, he noticed that the playground was once again devoid of kids. The "accident" must have occurred there. He didn't blame the school for keeping the kids inside.

The bleak desert landscape and barren rock formations outside his window made him miss the green rolling hills around Welton on Dormir. As the taxi-bot cruised down the highway, he nodded off for a moment, dreaming about Becky and the kids. A few seconds later, when he jerked awake, he wished he could just leave now and tell Norb there were no problems at Factory 309.

A robot greeted him at the hotel door and asked if he needed help with any luggage. Jake said he didn't and went straight to his room. He ordered a light supper and spent the rest of the night thinking about recent events. He hardly slept at all. He just couldn't shut off his mind. About an hour before dawn, he finally fell asleep, wishing he could contact his wife directly.

***

Early the next morning, Jake bought a sunhat with a drop-down visor in the hotel gift shop and headed for the park where he had met Ryan the day before. He kept his head down when he reached the park's entrance. He now knew it was monitored and didn't want to explain to anyone why he was here again.

Ryan was already sitting at the same bench on the walking trail, his shoulders hunched, his clothes rumpled, looking more than a little dejected. He wondered if Ryan and his friends might be sleeping outdoors somewhere nearby. Jake sat down on the bench across from him, pulled up his visor, and nodded. Before anyone spoke, a shadow crossed the space between them. Ryan's lookout must be close by.

"Have you fixed our problem yet?"

"It's more complicated than I thought," Jake said carefully. He had a feeling Ryan's gun could appear at any moment. He was still unarmed. If Ryan wanted to shoot, it would be a straight forward bloody deal.

"Okay, what do you need?" Ryan asked.

"I visited the factory yesterday, but they wouldn't let me anywhere near Building C-3. That's the place, isn't it? That's where you and your co-workers killed your supervisor, right?"

Ryan nodded.

"I need to get into that building. If we can prove your supervisor used a weapon that killed those GAP kids, they'll show leniency to you and your friends. They might even give you a promotion for helping to expose a corporate crime that is strictly prohibited by the government." Jake sighed. "But we have to prove it back at AWDCOR headquarters on Dormir."

While he was waiting for Ryan's response, Jake thought about the RS agent that was still in the local jail. Maybe he could get him involved. The RS Bureau's unspoken charter was to eradicate this kind of illegal corporate behavior.

"That makes sense," Ryan finally said, "but it's a long shot. Nobody has ever breached security at Factory 309 and lived to tell about it. You can't just go in and snoop around the CADS area. Even if you could somehow fake a gold skin tag, no one can easily hack into any design and test computer work stations."

"CADS? What's that?"

"I don't know what it means. I saw it on a design spec screen, but I don't know exactly what it stands for. It has something to do with that weapon." Ryan seemed to indicate a willingness to help, but he was obviously worried about any possibility of success.

"You must have co-worker friends who are still working in Building C-3. They must sympathize with your predicament. They could try to retrieve and copy the weapon's test data that was recorded when the children were killed."

"You smart guys don't know much, do you? Don't you think we would have thought of that? My co-worker friends are GAPS and only do assembly work. The techs are in charge of testing. GAPs aren't allowed access to weapon controls or design/test data files. Security increased in Building C-3 after those kids were killed. My co-workers can't make any unusual moves."

Jake frowned. "I see your point. Thanks for enlightening me. I'll have to think of something else." The RS agent in jail might hold the answer. Jake needed to contact him.

"By the way, Mr. Smart Investigator, our permanent skin tags aren't on our wrists. They're on the back of our necks. They'll automatically release a lethal toxin if we get anywhere near the factory's perimeter. They stopped using wrist tags for us after some guy went psycho in town and hurt a lot of people. His wrist tag was set to lethal if he ever returned to the factory. The guy just cut off the tag and caused a big fracas in the employee parking lot before the guards took him out." Ryan didn't reach for his weapon, but he was obviously angry that Jake didn't appear to have a viable plan.

As he walked back to the hotel, Jake wondered how the CEO would react if he knew illegal skin tags were in widespread use at one of his factories. In any case, the murder of GAP children by a company weapon would certainly get Mr. Milton's full attention.

Chapter 11

Jake decided to contact the RS Department first to try to get the RS agent released from the local jail. He couldn't just go there and inquire about him. That might stir up too much trouble, and he certainly had no inclination to go anywhere near that place again.

His message to the RS Department to alert them about the detained agent was returned by the government mail server with the message UNABLE TO PROCESS AT THIS TIME.

He decided to risk sending a coded message directly to the CEO. Maybe Mr. Milton had connections to the RS that might help him to spring the agent from jail. Mr. Milton probably still hadn't forgiven him for the shooting incident last month and might automatically delete his message—or worse—he might get Norb to fire him as soon as possible.

Mr. Milton:
   I suspect an illegal weapon is being

developed at Factory 309. It may be responsible for the deaths of several GAP children. There's an RS agent in the local jail that may be of assistance. Can you talk to the RS administrator about this? The agent might be able to help me.

Again, I'm very sorry about the incident last month.

Regards,
Jake

***

In his office, CEO Charles Milton read Jake's message and told his personal aide to set up a lunch meeting with Norb at the rooftop garden. Norb ran Factory 309. Maybe he knew something about a secret weapon program. The garden was a private area he used for meetings or just to take a break. It could be noisy at times, since it adjoined a sizable air drone pad, but he enjoyed the food, the exotic trees and plants, and the view of the surrounding city.

As usual, Norb wasn't on time, but Charles didn't care. The lunch-bots were serving his favorite foods, which included a spicy elongated sandwich, barbequed chips, and sun-dried apricots.

Just as he heard a drone take off from the nearby pad—and just as he was about to take a second bite of his lunch—he paused with his sandwich in midair. A tiny spot on the table, right next to his plate, seemed to be melting. The drone, which was now passing directly overhead at that very moment, made a strange sound. Even without looking up, Charles knew he was in trouble. He could already see the reflection of the flames on his plate. He dropped his sandwich and ducked under the table as the drone flamed past him, knocked over a lunch-bot, and crashed through the latticework surrounding the perimeter of the roof-top garden. When he heard screams from the street below, he hoped the drone's cargo didn't include live munitions and that its fuel pack would break apart in a fail-safe manner, minimizing the collateral damage.

The lunch-bots were still scurrying about, trying to make sense of what had happened, when Norb found him under the table.

"Mr. Milton—what's happening? Can I help?"

Charles got out from under the table and

brushed off his clothes. "No, I need to attend to some things right away. Go back to your office."

When Norb left, Charles reluctantly abandoned his lunch and left the rooftop garden. Whatever was going on, he knew Jake was in the middle of it, and maybe Norb was somehow involved. He needed a few minutes to regain his composure. Someone had tried to kill him. It had been pure luck that the drone flew over at that very instant and blocked the assassin's weapon.

He decided to take a different route through the building back to his office. It might be a good idea to vary his routine. As he navigated the longer distance past a number of clerk-bots and company offices, he kept thinking about Norb. How would he feel if he knew he had been chosen years ago to take over his position as CEO? Norb was one of the many abandoned infants that the company had taken in under its wings. But when DNA and IQ testing revealed Norb's superior genetics, Charles had stepped in and had altered the standard GAP regiment. He had quietly steered Norb's training along an executive business path. Norb had turned out well. He was aggressive, had the right superiority attitude, and treated his subordinates as property. Charles was thirty years older than Norb and had inherited his position many years ago when his father, the founder of AWDCOR, died from an assassin's attack. His father had run a tight ship but had been too lax on security. Charles hadn't made that same mistake and personally reviewed all security matters. He credited this attitude to his long tenure as CEO.

When he reached his office, Charles sat down at his desk screen and quickly accessed the full report on Edward Shaw's death. There seemed to be a similarity between it and what had just happened on the rooftop garden.

He made up his mind that Jake would get some help. The company supplied advanced and specialized weapons to the RS Department and other government agencies. Charles had many friends in high places who would help. In fact, they would be eager to offer assistance. Did they really have a choice? After all, some of the items AWDCOR had sold to them over the years would be grounds for criminal action if they leaked out to the news media.

Charles called the private com screen of the RS Department head and was surprised when William Thurst immediately began cursing at him, claiming that AWDCOR had murdered an RS team which had been sent to investigate a rumored illegal weapon system being built at Factory 309.

"You'll be held responsible for this, Charlie— and you damn well know what that means!" Before Charles could answer, the head of the RS added a few more choice cuss words and clicked off his screen.

Charles slumped in his chair and knew it would take all of his skills to get out of this mess. It was becoming clear that Factory 309 held the answers.

"Norb, get your gear ready and meet me at my ship's berth. Now! We have a mess to straighten out on Barros."

The ship was outfitted with extra large thrusters and would arrive at Barros in half the normal time.

Chapter 12

Jake was getting dressed when the com screen in his hotel room signaled a gold-status message was being received. Only the CEO himself could have sent such a message. He hoped it would be good news—he was getting nowhere in this investigation. His Brain Implant kept reminding him of the message he had received warning him to file a favorable report or his family would suffer. He hoped Becky and the kids were still safe.

The gold-status message was highly encrypted and took several seconds before Jake could read it.

Norbert and I will be arriving soon—Mr. Charles Milton

The CEO's short message indicated he was being extra cautious. Jake wondered if things were getting worse, or if something had happened to his family. No, they were probably fine. If they weren't, Norb would have left him some sort of short, ominous note. That would be Norb's usual style when dealing with family matters. Jake wasn't on good terms with Mr. Milton after accidentally shooting him last month, but he hoped he wasn't holding a grudge.

As he was going out the door, the com screen announced all guests were to immediately assemble in the dining room. Now what?

When he had almost reached the dining area, he noticed the hotel staff was also headed in that direction. Even the food chef was in the group. Something big was up.

"All guests will please pack up and be ready for transport to the AWDCOR civilian subcontractor hotel. All hotel employees will immediately convene in Conference Room A." The hotel administrator's voice was tense. He was obviously anxious about something.

Jake was going to protest but noticed that several security guards were gathering in the lobby. This wasn't a good time to be argumentative. He went back to his room, gathered up his few personal items, and headed back downstairs to check out.

"Thank you for your stay," the lobby droid told him. "I hope the accommodations were to your liking. Your transport is ready. Have a good day."

As the bus was driving away, Jake noticed more security police were arriving and checkpoints with armed barriers were being set up. The CEO was indeed coming to pay a visit. Mr. Milton's paranoia for security would actually tip off his enemies. They would know for sure now that he was going to show up. Jake couldn't blame the CEO for the enhanced security. His own idea of a low-key security team had obviously turned into a fiasco. Would he ever be allowed to forget that he had ended up shooting Mr. Milton and a bodyguard? Thankfully, his smart-gun only tranquilized him, and Ed had saved the day.

The subcontractor hotel was adequate. The rooms were all alike—sparse and utilitarian. As he passed the cafeteria, Jake could see it didn't have food-bots to wait on tables. You served yourself from a buffet. All the food was prepared by cook-bots and would undoubtedly vary from mediocre to disgusting.

After he settled into his room, Jake lay down on one of the double beds. He was exhausted and needed to rest. A few hours later, he found himself bolting upright from a sound sleep.

It was early morning. Someone was pounding

on the door, telling him to get dressed for a trip.

"What's up?" Jake asked the two guards when he opened the door.

"We don't actually know," one guard answered, "except you're to be escorted to Factory 309." Both guards were armed with PW-10 weapons. Jake wished he had his own PW-10 at his side.

The ride to Factory 309 was the same as before. This time children were playing outside when they passed by the GAP academy. They pulled over once to let a long convoy of AWDCOR heavy transports go by. Jake watched as the convoy drove to the factory's delivery entrance and disappeared into a warehouse.

"So, it's you again," the guard at the first guard shack said, sounding rather irritated.

They put him through the same routine as before—including the thorough body scan. "Leave all your pocket items here—plus your ear-com," the guard told him, as he hand-patted Jake from head to toe.

"Okay, take Mr. Safety Inspector in," the guard ordered Jake's escorts.

After they went through the tunnel, Jake's escorts stood by while he put his hand into the tagger at the second guard station.

"Enjoy your skin tag," the guard named Phil said with a grin.

Jake wondered what he meant by that. When he pulled out his hand, he was surprised to see a red skin tag blinking on his wrist.

"You know, of course, that your tag can be lethal. Be a good boy during your meeting." Phil laughed and motioned to another guard. "Take him and his escorts to the conference room in Building C-3. No detours."

The assembly area in Building C-3 was empty, except for a few large packing crates in one corner. When Jake entered the conference room, the three guards that had accompanied him waited outside. Norb and Mr. Milton were already in the room, sitting at a long table. Jake couldn't quite read the expression on the CEO's face, but he seemed to be nervous. Something was up.

Chapter 13

Mr. Milton didn't ask Jake to take a seat. He just looked him over, sizing him up as if he were a cut of raw meat ready to be sliced, diced, and fried. Norb finally broke the silence and told him to sit down. Although Jake wanted to ask Norb about his family, he knew better. Neither of these two men cared about such matters.

"So, Jake," Mr. Milton said, "we have a mess here. It appears you haven't helped at all and may actually be involved in some employee problems. Norb has assured me that no illegal weapons are being built at this factory. . . . But some disgruntled GAPs *have* killed their supervisor." The CEO's tone of voice was flat, as he tapped the table with one finger and glanced at Norb.

Norb chimed in. "Your Ryan buddy and friends have been captured and locked up by the local police."

Jake was now concerned he might not leave this room alive.

"This Ryan GAP," the CEO added, "admitted he talked to you. He gave the police some story about you trying to help. I'm disappointed you found it necessary to offer assistance to such a disreputable character."

They were both staring at him with their hands folded on the table, waiting for a response. Jake knew he had to play this straight, but he couldn't reveal the whole story.

"Yeah, I was using Ryan to help with my investigation. He gave me some information in confidence that I needed to follow up on. I was only doing my job to expedite my assignment as quickly as possible."

"You know, Jake," Mr. Milton said, "you always know how to say the right things. Too bad that William Thurst is after me. You know of him, don't you? Yes, I'm sure you do. He's the head of the RS. Well, I need to throw him a sacrificial turkey. This turkey has to be smart enough to be capable of doing bad things."

The CEO turned to Norb while he continued talking. "I think we've solved AWDCOR's problem with the RS Department. We'll just hand Jake over to their enforcers and let the police take care of the wayward GAP employees."

As Norb was nodding in agreement, Mr.

Milton pressed a red button on a com device that he kept in his vest pocket. The three guards who had been waiting in the hall came into the room with a prisoner transfer chair in tow. Without saying a word, they yanked Jake to his feet and slammed him into the chair.

Jake wasn't thinking about himself when his arms and legs were clamped into place. He could only think about Becky and the kids. The RS enforcers were known for quick and quiet executions. His family would be thrown into the street—or worse.

As Jake was being rolled out of the room, he heard Norb ask Mr. Milton when they would be leaving for Dormir. The door closed behind him before he could hear the answer.

At the guard station, Jake was glad they removed his red skin tag. At least they hadn't decided to invoke its lethal mode.

"I guess we won't be bothered with you again," Phil said with a laugh, as the guards steered Jake into the back of a police transport.

Chapter 14

The ride to the police station was fast, in spite of a dust storm. No one had locked Jake's prisoner chair into place when they put him in the police transport van. He spent the entire time slamming back and forth from one end of the paddy wagon to the other as they sped down the highway. When he started to yell for them to stop to secure his chair, he heard laughter coming from the front of the vehicle. He didn't say anything then. He just endured another roll and slam across the length of the wagon and kept his mouth shut. These guys knew exactly what they were doing.

When his prisoner chair was maneuvered into a jail cell, one of the guards was still smirking. A wall screen displayed his case status: *Rogue executive awaiting RS transfer to Dormir*. That was a joke. Jake knew from his past employment with the RS that the transfer team would make sure he had an unplanned excursion into deep space on the trip home. That was their favorite method of dealing with his kind. Deep space was a perfect dumping ground.

The guards left his arms and legs cuffed to the prisoner chair and slammed the cell door shut. Unable to move anything but his head, Jake looked around the confined space and wondered what was happening to Becky and the kids at this very moment. He hoped they were all right. There was nothing to do now but wait for the RS agents to arrive. This was the worst situation in his life, but he wouldn't lose hope. In spite of everything, he was still breathing. How much time did he have left? Were they going to torture him—just a little—before they dumped him into space? If it weren't for Becky and the kids, he would be looking for a permanent way out of this before they had the chance to do that.

Jake snapped out of his bleak mood when his Brain Implant signaled another BI was nearby. With nothing to lose, he tried to initiate a BI contact. It was no surprise that the same RS agent he had encountered before responded. Why was he still around? Maybe there was hope after all. Jake immediately messaged a thought to him.

What's going on there? Jake couldn't prevent his message from including some images of his family and the last meeting with Mr. Milton and

Norb.

The agent immediately responded. *I sense you're in a jam. You should really try to work on your BI thought processes.*

Jake noted the agent's message was clear with no mind clutter. Before he could answer, the agent messaged him again. *I've never been charged with any crime. A team from the RS is coming to take me back home. I don't understand why the police won't release me now so I can get cleaned up and get some new clothes. A woman likes to look her best when she's traveling.*

Jake took all this in. He didn't tell this woman that the same RS agents were coming for him to give him a "special" space trip. It was odd the RS agent was still being confined and isolated. Jake was going to make a last-ditch effort. He might get this agent in trouble and himself killed, but that was going to happen anyway.

Hey, RS agent, I think you'd better tell me what you know about CADS. I know there's some bad stuff going on. I'll try to get you released ASAP. This last part was doubtful, to say the least. He hoped his BI wouldn't convey that.

You must be one of the investigators we heard

AWDCOR was dispatching to Factory 309. The agent hesitated for a few seconds, as if sorting something out in her mind, and then continued. *I'm a RS-20 agent and was the outside lookout when our team infiltrated Factory 309 last week.*

Jake was impressed they got that far.

They obtained data, she continued, *about CADS. The data was sent to me, and I recorded it. AWDCOR is developing an illegal weapon and accidentally caused the deaths of five children during its testing. The RS team leader told me to leave the area and report back to headquarters ASAP. We were only a snoop team—not enforcers. The team leader's last message to me was RUN! GET OUT OF HERE! SECURITY IS ON TO US! THEY'RE CLOSING THE TUNNEL DOORS! I haven't seen or heard from my team again.*

Jake told the RS-20 agent he understood her completely and messaged that he would see what he could do to help, which, of course, was absolutely nothing while he was strapped to a prisoner chair. He hoped he kept that thought out of his message. Sadly, he knew exactly what had happened to her teammates. They had undoubtedly been cremated in that tunnel.

Jake's cell screen suddenly came on with

Norb's smiling face.

"I never liked you, Jake—always caring about other people—a totally poor attitude for this company." On the screen, Jake could see Norb leaning back in a flight chair, gloating and enjoying this one-way conversation. "I had your family moved to my own special hideaway. Too bad your silly dog was killed in the process."

Jake looked away. He wouldn't give Norb the pleasure of seeing the tears in his eyes. *You son of a bitch—* He gritted his teeth. "What have you done to my family?"

"Enjoy your trip back, Jake. Too bad my associate killed Edward. But I'll take the blame for that. I wasn't specific enough when I put in my request. You were supposed to be the target. Anyway, maybe you'll get lucky and have a lady join you on your last journey." Norb suddenly frowned, realizing he needed to stop talking. A moment later, the screen went blank.

Jake was right—RS-20 was in danger too. She had to be the lady Norb was referring to. Someone had bought off a team of RS enforcer agents. This was starting to make sense. RS-20's recording would incriminate AWDCOR and would expose others that were involved. How was he going to convince RS-20 she was in danger? She was a career RS agent who trusted her department. She certainly wouldn't think they would intentionally harm her. How could he convince her things weren't as they appeared?

Even before he contacted her through his BI, Jake knew she wouldn't believe him. After a long exchange of mind messages, including a summary of everything Norb had just told him, she finally fell silent and abruptly ended their conversation.

Jake sighed and then suddenly struggled against the straps and cuffs that were holding him tight to the prisoner chair. It was no use. He couldn't move anything but his head. It was going to be a long night.

Chapter 15

The next morning, when the RS agents came for Jake and maneuvered his prisoner chair out of the cell, they didn't say anything to him or to each other. He was surprised he could only detect faint, unintelligible thoughts from them. Maybe they had Enhanced Brain Implants. Those were only rumored to exist, but their selective coding would keep their BI thoughts from prying minds like his. RS-20 was a high-level agent. Could she read these selective BI units? Hopefully, she could and would deduce that things were not as they appeared.

The two RS agents kept Jake confined to the prisoner chair as they loaded him into a van. An attractive, middle-aged woman with dark, shoulder-length hair was already sitting in one of the row seats toward the front, along with several members of the RS team. When she turned to study Jake for a moment, her intelligent-looking green eyes reminded him of Becky. She seemed to be happy, even though her clothes were dirty and torn. If this was RS-20, her happiness would be short-lived.

As they drove to the spaceport, Jake's BI detected only low-level bits of conversation from the RS agents. He noticed RS-20 didn't seem to be in the loop. He smiled to himself. These guys may not be so clever after all. Jake sent a thought via his BI to test his theory.

A bomb has been attached to this vehicle. I'll disarm it if you release me now.

RS-20 was the only one that jerked around to stare at him. The other RS agents didn't bat an eye. Could RS-20 even communicate with this RS team through her BI? He guessed she couldn't.

He knew RS-20 wouldn't take his bomb threat too seriously. She would only wonder about his IQ. Corporate and government vehicles were equipped with explosive and bio-hazards sensors that would trigger alarms which could be heard and seen a city block away. You couldn't even get close to these vehicles with those types of weapons. The vehicle's sensors not only sniffed the air but also used gamma and low-level x-rays. They didn't deter all attacks, but they made it very difficult to attach anything dangerous to a vehicle.

Jake had to convince RS-20 of her impending

danger. He wondered if she knew that this team wasn't the usual RS transport crew and that he was going to be killed in space.

RS-20 nudged the agent sitting next to her. "I think your prisoner back there may try something stupid. You may need my help. Can I have my com unit back? Maybe a weapon?"

"Yeah, this guy is more dangerous than you know. He was complicit in the death of your team and is involved with child killers." The agent hesitated a few seconds, obviously receiving a BI message from someone in the van. "We don't have any spare PW-2s or ear-coms, and your com device was broken by the cops. You'll get a new one back at the office. We're sorry your BI doesn't work with us, but we're on a high-level assignment. You don't have clearance to know about it."

"Yeah—okay—I can wait until we get home," RS-20 answered in a flat tone. A second later, she spoke up again, obviously trying to change the subject. "Do you mind if we stop at a department store for a second to get me some new clothes?"

"Sorry, but we're on a tight schedule."

Does that make any sense to you? Jake

reasoned with her. *They might not have time to stop at a store, but why won't they give you a weapon? Don't RS-20 agents have clearance just below the department head? Don't RS teams working with dangerous prisoners always have replacement weapons and com units available?*

After Jake sent his message, RS-20 stared straight ahead and remained silent. Good. Maybe she was starting to think he was telling the truth. Maybe she might realize these guys were up to something.

A few minutes later, as they were going through the first gate at the spaceport, RS-20 finally answered him.

Okay. I'll need details. We'll talk later.

Chapter 16

After passing through the spaceport security check points, they drove to the launch pad where their ship was supposed to be. It wasn't there.

"It figures," the driver said.

"AWDCOR ship control!" another team member yelled into his com device. "Where the hell is our ship?"

As soon as he finished speaking, a medium-sized AWDCOR transport ship with a new paint job began rolling over to their launch pad.

"Okay, I understand." The RS team member who had yelled a few moments ago shook his head in disgust at the guy sitting next to him. "You had orders to repaint," he said into his com. "I see it now. I wish somebody would keep me advised of these things. Team, let's get moving!"

They didn't waste any time boarding the transport ship. As Jake was moved to the ship's open-air loading elevator, he noticed a familiar chemical odor. This transport smelled just like the ship that had blown up on its descent to Barros.

They loaded Jake into an large airlock on a lower deck and bolted his prisoner chair to the floor. That was nice of them. At least he was secured in place and wouldn't be slammed around on take-off. RS-20 and another RS agent were seated in flight chairs nearby.

Should I tell you the whole story? Jake asked her through his BI.

I'm listening.

Jake started from the beginning, keeping everything as concise as possible and trying to keep all thoughts of Becky and the kids from cluttering his message. He wasn't entirely successful with that. When he saw the countdown screen, he realized it was Lucy's 6th birthday. Was she even still alive?

After he had quickly summarized everything that had happened from the time he and Ed had received the threat at work last week, RS-20 began asking questions.

That threat you received—what exactly did it say? Do you still have the BI recording?

Yes, he messaged, as he quickly retrieved it and relayed it to her. *You w-will file a favorable report on Factory 309 or your families w-will suffer.*

RS-20 turned pale. Jake wasn't sure it was

because of the message he had sent to her or because the ship's engines were beginning to warm up.

Are you okay?

It took a moment for RS-20 to compose herself. *Michael Nash—the personal assistant to the RS Department head—talks like that. He stutters on any word that begins with the letter W.* She paused for a second before she continued. *I've been good friends with the head of the RS, William Thurst, for a long time. Bill is aggressive, but he wouldn't allow innocents to be harmed. He can't be involved.*

Are you sure? Jake asked.

Absolutely. This RS team obviously doesn't realize they won't be around for long after they kill us. Michael is a real bastard. He's undoubtedly working with your boss on a sinister deal.

The ship's screen announced that lift-off was in progress. The engines were starting to ramp up to full thrust.

What do we do now, Jake?

We've got to take over the ship.

RS-20 laughed out loud and then quickly bowed her head and pretended to be checking her flight harness. The RS agent next to her glanced at her and frowned. Maybe he hadn't heard her laugh over the sound of the engines.

Jake, she messaged with her head still down, *how are you going to take on an RS team while you're strapped to a prisoner chair?*

He ignored her question. He was still thinking about her assessment that the whole team would be killed. *So you think they'll all be killed after they kill us?*

Michael Nash is ruthless, she answered. *He won't want to leave any trace of what he's doing. I warned Bill about this guy. I kept telling him he was dangerous, but he always said he needed hard evidence to justify firing him.*

I wonder how they're going to get rid of a high-level RS agent like you? Maybe they plan to leave you nearby when they open the air hatch to dump me. It will probably be listed as an accident. . . . RS-20, we have a bigger problem. Even if we avoid being killed in outer space, I'm sure the crypsis camo system on this transport has been sabotaged. It's going to burn up when we try to land. That's what happened to my last ship. But this time, I'll bet the ejection units have been sabotaged. No one's getting off this ship alive.

RS-20 was silent for over a minute, as the ship fired its final rockets that would propel them into outer space.

I just thought of something, she finally said through her BI. *They told me my ear-com was broken, but I think it's okay. It was set up to work only with my genetic coding. I know it must be on board—it's too important to leave with the police. The team's findings are recorded on it. Maybe I can—*

Jake interrupted her BI message. *RS-20, can you give me more details on your team's infiltration?*

*Okay—sure. The team posed as a group of subcontractors working on robotic system upgrades with permission to enter Building C-3 at Factory 309. I was dressed like a field botanist and stayed out of sight near the GAP academy. Somebody tipped off security. The team—*RS-20 hesitated, obviously trying to gain her composure—*the team was caught in a tunnel. I haven't heard from them since. A police drone ordered me to stop while I was running away from the area. When the police officers arrived, they didn't believe I was there to study the cactus. I was* *lucky they weren't AWDCOR security. They told me I was trespassing in a restricted GAP training area and would have to be detained until they could verify who I was.*

Jake could see the tension and exhaustion in RS-20's face. The reality of their situation was obviously getting to her. Their only hope for survival was to switch the RS team to their side as soon as possible. If they could do that, they could work together and figure out a way to land the ship without activating the deadly crypsis system.

Jake wondered why Michael Nash had arranged that he and RS-20 be killed in space. Why not let the sabotaged ship take care of everyone at once? After a moment's reflection, he knew exactly why. Michael Nash didn't want this RS team to be suspicious of anything. They were following Standard Operating Procedure to the letter. The SOP for rogue employees was a one-way trip in space. If they didn't do that, the team would face disciplinary action. Such a blatant disregard for standard procedures would make them wonder what was going on. These guys didn't realize they were going to be killed as well. But maybe he and RS-20 could reason with the team leader. Maybe he was a sensible person. If he seemed a bit brutal for taking them into space to be dumped, he was only following orders. Jake had no doubt he would carry out those orders without hesitation. Unless—

RS-20, we need to have a chat with the RS team leader ASAP. Let's tell him the ship's ejection systems aren't functional. I'm convinced they won't work. If that turns out to be the case, they may believe us when we tell them we're not the only ones who are going to die on this trip.

If the ejection systems were inoperative, Jake knew they couldn't be fixed. The team leader would know that as well. Jake's chair was occupying the space a repair-bot would normally be located. Nobody on board had the expertise to repair delicate and somewhat dangerous ejection systems.

The agent seated next to RS-20 suddenly noticed her worried look.

"Lady, are you getting space sick? I don't want to clean up any mess."

"I'm a little nervous about that prisoner."

The agent laughed. "Don't worry about him," he smirked. "You'll be just fine."

"Maybe it would help if I could talk to your

team leader," RS-20 suggested politely.

"Lenny's busy right now, but I'll let him know."

The ship engine's throttled back. They had left the atmosphere of Barros and were headed for Dormir.

Chapter 17

Wow—he sure looks young, RS-20 messaged to Jake, when the team leader came through the hatch.

Lenny was tall, red-headed, and obviously in love with himself, wearing short sleeves in space to show off an intricate network of tattoos on his muscled arms.

Yeah, Jake agreed, *he must be a GAP that the RS hired from a private company.*

"I understand you wanted to talk. Make it quick—I'm busy." Lenny's tattoos on his lower right arm suddenly changed and flashed snakes biting each other.

Jake could see that RS-20 was trying not to frown. "You should let me try to fix my ear-com," she said pleasantly. "It's secured by my DNA imprint and a level 9 password. It's of no use to anyone else."

Jake was listening to this conversation carefully and wondered what RS-20 was up to. Government com units were highly secured and would sometimes self-destruct if anyone tampered with them.

"Yeah, why not?" His tats flashed question marks as he added with a smile, "There may be something on it that will prove useful to me in the future. I'll have somebody fetch it—we'll use the wall screen here."

RS-20—be careful. This Lenny character is sporting a tattoo system that costs a fortune. I always wanted one, but Becky wouldn't hear of it. Our savings will barely pay for our kids' advanced education. This guy must be on the take.

"What's on your com unit?" Lenny asked while they were waiting.

"Oh, you know," RS-20 answered casually, "just the usual stuff—and a private file."

Jake suppressed a smile. He knew what she was doing. The team leader's interest would automatically focus on that private file, hoping it contained things he could use to blackmail or ruin someone in high places.

When Lenny grinned, his tats displayed daggers with jewels. "I can't wait for you to download your files to the wall screen."

I think Lenny's lust for power and influence will be his undoing, Jake said through his BI.

As RS-20 was nodding in agreement, the hatch opened. A team member handed Lenny an ear-com that was scratched and dirty.

"Okay, lady, here's your com. Activate it and set it to display on the wall screen."

"Give me a few seconds. It needs to be rebooted."

The entire RS team was watching the ship's com screens now. RS-20's files came into view: Contact lists, memos, and a locked file.

"Excellent," Lenny quipped. "Unlock that file." As he spoke, his tat on his left arm began displaying a hangman's noose.

"Oh," RS-20 said, "you don't want to see that. It's just boring company stuff."

Jake laughed to himself. Nobody on the ship would buy that whopper of a lie.

Lenny's tats changed to a person being strangled in various shades of blue. "Quit fooling around, lady. Unlock it—NOW."

When RS-20 complied, the file opened and revealed a laser-like weapon mounted inside a substantial camo drone. The design specs and test data were shown as sub-menus.

"This is boring," somebody said. Everyone had

obviously been hoping for some visual entertainment on this trip. Lenny reached out to finger the exit icon but apparently changed his mind and hit the Test Data sub-menu instead.

As the file opened, it showed the weapon inside the drone being energized. A slight ionization emerged from it. In a micro-second, children laughing and playing tag on the ground below were burned up in a blue flame. Nothing remained but small piles of ashes, which soon mixed with the dust and scattered with the wind.

Nobody said anything for several seconds. Lenny's tat system went offline as he considered what he had observed.

"Hey, Lenny, what's going on here?" a team member finally asked. "She obviously received this recording from her team. What's AWDCOR up to? We can't dispose of her—she's practically a witness to the crime. Geez—killing kids is a big-time capital offense. Just knowing about it means lifetime duty cleaning up space debris."

"Shut up! I've got to think this out."

Jake was also shaken. Now he understood exactly how Ed and his father had died.

Chapter 18

Jake and RS-20 knew their lives would be determined by what Lenny said next.

"Okay, I don't understand why this lady's recording shows this. But I'm not going against orders just because of this one thing. What difference does it make? We were going to eject all their personal effects with them anyway—including the com unit."

Jake's eyes met RS-20's. Her face was still perfectly composed, but they both knew it was over.

RS-20, Lenny's GAP training won't allow him to disobey orders easily. Maybe I can rattle him. Let me try. . . .

"Before you carry out your cowardly act," Jake said as casually as possible, "you might consider this: Murdering an RS-20 agent is a capital offense. You and your team will be caught and punished."

"We'll risk it," Lenny laughed, as his tats began displaying piles of gold credits.

"You're assuming this ship will land safely," Jake interjected. "I noticed it has a new camo and paint job. It was put on at the AWDCOR shipyard not long before we lifted off, right?"

"Yeah, so what?" Lenny's tats hadn't changed. They were still showing piles of gold credits.

"This ship will land on Dormir—but only as a flaming mass of debris. Nobody will be risking anything after that, Mr. Team Leader."

"Right," Lenny said cynically, as his tats started flashing a firing squad shooting a prisoner. "Next you'll be telling me you have some divine power to stop it from happening if we release you."

"The crypsis camo system on this ship has been modified to start burning when it enters an atmosphere. I should know—my last ship crashed because of it. . . . My new partner died."

Another RS team member suddenly spoke up. "Lenny, there might be something to this. I heard some rumors about a sneaky new way to take out ships when they land. I don't think we should ignore him. I saw it on the news—this guy's ship was on fire before it crashed."

"I'll do the thinking here!" Lenny replied and then fell silent. Jake could tell he was giving instructions to his team through his BI. At least he had managed to buy them some time.

"Lenny," RS-20 said, "you'd better check the ejection systems. Sounds like you may need them."

"I'm not stupid. I just told my guys to do that." His tats were not active.

Good one, RS-20. I think he's starting to worry—his tat system has gone offline.

After a few minutes passed, Lenny lowered his head slightly, but Jake could see how pale his face had become. "Okay, everybody," he ordered, "go back to the command compartment! Leave the lady agent here. I'll keep an eye on her."

When the last team member had closed the hatch, Lenny swiveled around in his chair to face Jake. "Okay, Mr. Prisoner, what's the deal with this new camo paint? Come on! We don't have much time. . . . Like you said, the ejection units aren't functional—"

"Sorry, Lenny, you and your team are involved in something that's above your pay grade. I have no idea how to save the ship. And even if we somehow survive, there are more things to consider. So, Mr. Smart Team Leader, what do you do now?"

That ought to panic him, but what ARE we going to do, Jake? Lenny's good at following orders, but he can't make decisions.

While Lenny was obviously struggling to think of a solution, Jake smiled at him. "Lenny, this paint is designed to burn when it encounters an atmosphere. It's going to burn, no matter what. Maybe we can ignite it here in space. It shouldn't burn too hot without oxygen. Or maybe we could try landing in a place with no atmosphere, like a moon."

"You're nuts! We can't go out there and try to burn off the camo paint in space. You don't know for sure what it's gonna do once it's ignited. And we don't have enough fuel to make it to any airless moons. . . . Why are you smiling like that, lady? Do you have any better ideas?"

RS-20's slight smile suddenly turned into a wide grin. "As a matter of fact, Lenny—I do."

Chapter 19

"I was anticipating you would need my help, Lenny," RS-20 said sweetly. "As you know, I'm a Grade 20 agent. I have experience in situations like this."

"Lenny, how about letting me out of this damn chair?" Jake complained, struggling for a moment against his restraints. "I need to stretch. My arms, legs, and back are hurting like hell."

"Not yet," Lenny answered, "maybe after we hear the lady's idea." He paused to flick a switch on the panel in front of him. "My guys up in the command deck need to hear this."

Jake sighed and sank back into his chair.

"Lenny, you're young, inexperienced, and overly ambitious." RS-20 didn't add that he was also a pawn easy to control with money. "Please pay attention as I tell you what we should do."

Lenny frowned but didn't say anything.

"I'm guessing we're about 2 hours away from Dormir," RS-20 continued, "and the ship is on autopilot." When Lenny was silent, she raised one eyebrow at him and waited for his response.

"Yeah, sounds right."

"Okay. We need to get off this ship before the final approach to Dormir. Any call for a rescue ship will be intercepted by Michael Nash. He's going to issue instructions to destroy this transport."

Lenny's tats remained offline, but he had begun to blink his eyes much too rapidly. "Uh, why would he do that?"

"Oh, Lenny, you're so young—so naïve. You and your team know too much. Even you should be aware of that. When the order is given to destroy a ship hijacked by a dangerous prisoner, no one will even question it." RS-20 paused to brush a wayward hair from her eyes, but Jake had the feeling she only did that to stop herself from smacking Lenny across his face. "We don't want to do anything that will raise alarms on Dormir. Okay, Lenny, I want you to send a brief text message to your associate on Dormir that your mission was completed. Tell him everything went as planned."

"I still haven't heard how we're going to get out of this, but I was going to send a message like that anyway."

"Good. . . . I need to be in the control flight console to complete this properly. Let's both go up there together and get this done."

"Don't forget about me!" Jake called out, as she and Lenny made their way toward the hatch.

RS-20 looked back at him and winked. "Don't worry, Jake, you'll be playing a key role in this."

***

After Lenny sent his message stating that their mission was completed and everything had gone according to plan, RS-20 switched off the ship-to-planet com and adjusted the ship-to-ship com for voice only. She ignored Lenny's worried look as she disengaged the autopilot and camo system.

"You know it's dangerous to turn off the camo in this area of space."

"Yes, Lenny, dear, I know all about space pirates," she answered, as she began to switch the engine's power off and on in a random fashion.

RS-20, I can feel the ship's thrusters cycling off and on. What's happening up there?

Were setting the bait, RS-20 answered Jake through her BI. *I hope it's noticed.*

"Now what happens?" Lenny asked.

"We just wait," RS-20 replied. "It won't be long now if anyone's monitoring this traffic zone."

RS-20, I'm watching the ship's status and com screen. Are you sure about this tactic?

She didn't have time to answer Jake's question.

"Ship in distress, we have observed that your engines are failing. Do you need assistance?" The automated masculine voice was seductively smooth—too smooth.

"We do need help!" RS-20 answered shrilly. "Our main drive is erratic! Other systems have gone offline, including the ejection units! You have to help us!"

"Ship in distress, we need to know more before we can proceed to help. Who are you, and what is your cargo?"

RS-20 smiled to herself and then at Lenny. They had a pirate on the hook.

"Rescue ship, our ship is AWDCOR SC-27 out of Barros. We're transporting a wounded VIP to Dormir for emergency medical needs. We have a seven-person medical and security team on board—no other cargo."

"SC-27, please turn on your landing lights and

turn off all thrusters. We will dock with you in 7 minutes."

When the com fell silent, RS-20 moved quickly, unlatching her harness and making her way toward the hatch. "Jake," she called out to the com screen, "you're the VIP with a spinal injury. Lenny, take over here while I go down and hook Jake up to a med kit. Tell your team to do nothing rash when they dock and come aboard. Don't mess with the ship's controls. I've set the autopilot and engines to come back on a few minutes after we exit and close the docking hatch."

"I don't think it matters what we do," Lenny answered sullenly. "This pirate is just gonna space us and take the ship."

"Lenny," Jake scolded him through the com screen, "you really should learn more about making deals. I'm sure this pirate won't want a small transport that can be easily traced when they can ransom an AWDCOR VIP."

***

A few moments later, RS-20 and a team member were letting Jake out of his chair.

"Oh, man, I wasn't sure I'd be able to move again."

"Enjoy it," RS-20 told him, "after we finish modifying this to look like a medical chair, you'll have to return and play the wounded VIP."

Jake stretched his arms and legs several times and then moved around to look out through the viewport. A drone that was twice as big as their ship was starting to become faintly visible. Its camo system wasn't a top-line unit, but it was good enough to thwart unwanted detection.

A minute later, he reluctantly returned to the chair as RS-20 hooked a med kit to his wrist.

"If anyone asks," RS-20 told him, "you were hurt during a weapon demo on Barros. I'll play medic, and Lenny's team will be your security detail. Jake, it will be up to you to negotiate a deal and. . . ." RS-20 stopped, startled by the jolt of the pirate drone docking to their ship. "We use our BIs from now on."

Chapter 20

The drone ship was well armed. Jake was glad they hadn't provoked a fight. The escape hatch status screen signaled the docking connection was successfully attached and pressures between the drone and their transport ship were now equalized.

"Well, here goes," RS-20 said, pushing the open button on the hatch.

An illegal gun-bot was already waiting for them, pointing its weapons directly at them. "Please line up side by side," the gun-bot said. "Tell the others to come down to this area for inspection."

I sure hope Lenny and his team don't try anything, RS-20 messaged to Jake. He nodded in agreement.

While the gun-bot waited for the others, it assumed a defensive position. One of its many cameras inspected Jake's face closely.

"You are Jake Worthington, an AWDCOR investigator, not a VIP. Please explain."

Jake wondered how he was going to talk his

way out of this one. This pirate was smarter than the ones he had encountered during his days with the RS.

"Jake, play along—tell them you are AWDCOR's top security chief and are on the CEO's staff. That makes you a VIP."

"Look," Jake said, "I'm on the CEO's staff. I have to—" He stopped to twitch and moan for effect before he continued, "I—I have to get my spine fixed ASAP. I'm sure we can come to an arrangement."

On the com screen, they could see two more sensor-bots had boarded and were already beginning a thorough search of every nook and cranny of their ship with a sophisticated array of detectors and molecular penetrating analyzers. As they continued their search, an icon with a skull and cross-bones suddenly flashed on the main com screen.

"Let's keep this simple," someone announced. It was the same male voice that had offered them assistance before. "Have your CEO pay 5 million credits, and we'll see what we can do to help you."

"Let's make it 1 million credits, payable right after you land us safely."

Jake, you like to live on the edge. RS-20

messaged to him.

Not really—but these guys expect to negotiate.

"Lenny—," RS-20 whispered, "don't even think about it."

"We could take out that gun-bot," Lenny whispered back, "there are more of us, you know."

"Wouldn't work," a team member next to him said under his breath. "That pirate drone would just destroy this ship and leave."

Then Lenny did something stupid. He started to draw his PW-2 from his holster.

The gun-bot spun around. A compartment door in its side sprung open and released a swarm of tiny drones. They buzzed and swirled in unison around their heads for a moment before they suddenly dispersed in groups of five, homing in on each person.

"What the heck?" Jake asked, as one of the drones attached itself to his neck, and another four latched onto each of his limbs.

"Those are my special home-built sting-on-command wasp drones," the pirate's voice announced with a laugh. "Their sting is lethal on my order. So, let's play nice. Okay?"

Lenny's hand dropped from his holster as he

nervously eyed the wasp drones on his arms and legs. Jake had the feeling his tat system would be spelling out YIPES if it came back online at that moment.

A full minute passed before they heard the pirate's voice again.

"My bots have checked out your ship. I don't really buy your story about transporting Jake Worthington for emergency medical treatment, but I've dealt with his partner in the past. Ed Shaw always treated me right. Let's make it 2 million in open credits, right after you land. I'll be letting you off at a nice, quiet place—far from the main spaceport."

Jake breathed a sigh of relief. So, Ed—even dead—had saved his skin once again.

The sensor and gun-bots left their ship and returned to the drone.

"Your group needs to get moving," the pirate said. "Please board my drone ship now," he added politely, just as the skull and cross-bones icon on the main com screen went dark.

"You pulled it off, Jake," RS-20 said, while she was maneuvering his chair through the airlock and into the pirate's drone.

"We still have some problems to face, but my

dead partner gets most of the credit." Ed must have done something big for this pirate in the past.

As Lenny followed his team through the hatch, he hit the auto-latch button to close the door behind him. That would activate RS-20's program in the navi-computer to continue its voyage to Dormir on autopilot. The pirate had no use for their ship. He was only interested in their money.

The drone ship retracted the docking assembly and turned in the direction of Dormir.

RS-20, I don't trust Lenny. He may try to make a side deal with this pirate.

I agree. Leave him to me. I'll cut a deal with Lenny before we land.

Good. Before I forget, tell him to leave his tat system off. Who knows what that gun-bot might do if his arms start flashing.

Leave everything to me, Jake. I know he'll like what I'm going to propose.

"Hey, Lenny," she called out, "let's sit together back here. I'd like to have a little private chat with you."

Chapter 21

The sun was rising on Dormir when the camouflaged drone ship began landing in a remote rural area. Jake scanned the horizon through a viewport from his chair, wishing he knew where his family was. He couldn't try to contact Becky anytime soon. That might prove to be too dangerous if she and the kids were being held by Norb or his cronies.

Well, RS-20, we're back on Dormir. Now I have to find a way to make good on 2 million credits.

Before RS-20 could reply, a sensor-bot near them activated, retrieved a clear bag from one of its compartments, and moved toward the exit hatch.

"Set your weapons to SAFE," the pirate's voice ordered them, "and turn off your ear-coms." It was the first time they had heard from the pirate since they had begun their trip home. "You can leave my ship after you place everything in the bag. Don't miss anything. If you do, the bot will detect it. Don't forget—those wasps attached to you may seem docile right now, but they're ready to sting on my command."

Sounds like we'll be on solid ground in a minute, Jake.

Yeah—I hope I can locate my family soon.

When the drone ship landed, the exit hatch opened, and the gun-bot turned to face them.

"Exit now," it ordered. "Walk to a safe distance. The ship will be departing in 2 minutes." The gun-bot followed them through the hatch with its multiple weapons pointed at them. "Keep moving."

A minute later, when Jake looked back from his prisoner chair, he could see only a faint outline of the drone ship as it powered its engines and took off in a swirling blast of dirt and leaves. Within a few seconds, he could no longer see the ship at all. Not bad for a camo unit that wasn't even the top of its line.

The whole group stood around Jake's chair. The gun-bot was still positioned nearby, covering them with its array of weapons. They could hear something coming down the road in the distance, but RS-20 saw it first. A medium-sized transport was heading their way. It too had a camo system.

"Let me see. Move out of my way," Jake said from his chair, straining to look. "Oh, shit. That's an AWDCOR HV-5 rising from its roof. It can kill us all in less than a second. How did the pirate get one of those?"

The HV-5 was tracking them as the vehicle moved closer.

It stopped a few dozen paces from them. When the rear ramp dropped down, another gun-bot emerged, followed by a young blonde woman dressed in a pink T-shirt and faded jeans. She stayed behind the gun-bot as it came toward them. The transport moved to one side, giving it a clear shooting path.

"Lenny," RS-20 said, "tell your guys not to try anything. They wouldn't have bothered to bring us here if we were to be killed." RS-20's voice was firm but nervous.

"But it's only a *girl*," Lenny muttered under his breath. When he saw the look on RS-20's face, he clamped his mouth shut.

"Okay," the girl said, as she emerged from behind the gun-bot and came closer to them. "I know who Jake is. I'm guessing the rest of you are some sort of government agents. Let's get down to business. Jake has to fulfill his end of our bargain before we can proceed."

So, this is our pirate, RS-20 messaged to Jake. *She may be young, but she's not inexperienced.*

Agreed. Translation: I get the credits now, or we all die.

"Okay," Jake said aloud, "I'll need a com screen that can access AWDCOR headquarters."

The young woman gave a voice command to the gun-bot near her. When it slid out a small com screen, she motioned for RS-20 to bring Jake closer in his chair.

"I'm watching you, Jake," the girl told him. "Don't touch anything on the screen that doesn't meet my approval."

Jake was hoping Norb hadn't deleted his password to the AWDCOR special funds account. Surely it had slipped his mind. After all, Jake was supposed to be floating in deep space by now.

He was in luck. Within a few moments, he was able to access the special funds account. It usually received credits from under-the-table arms deals, but it was also used to speed up business transactions in a direct way. He hoped nobody would notice the 2 million withdrawal. It was in the range of normal bribe payouts, so it probably wouldn't attract any attention.

Jake touched the icon to finish the transaction. "There you go. Two million credits have been sent to this com. Now what?"

"Now we find out if we get to live," RS-20 said aloud.

The pirate motioned them back from the com screen before she stepped forward and touched the screen several times. "Okay. We're done here. . . . By the way," she added, as she began walking back to the ramp at the rear of her transport, "I've recorded this entire scene. It may prove useful to me in the future."

The gun-bot that had accompanied her swung its weapons away from them and followed her, while the other gun-bot came closer to them, still pointing its weapons directly at them. Jake was just starting to get rather nervous when the wasp drones suddenly detached themselves from everyone in the group. They buzzed around their heads several times before they suddenly swarmed together and flew into an open compartment in the gun-bot. A moment later, the gun-bot spun around and followed the pirate and the other bot into the transport.

The HV-5 kept its aim on them for a few more

seconds before it was lowered into the roof of the vehicle. The transport revved its engine, initiated its camo unit, and disappeared in front of them. When they heard it backing off and driving away, they couldn't see anything but a trail of dust and the pirate's hand as she threw a bag out of the window.

Chapter 22

"Lenny, while RS-20 unhooks me from this chair, go pick up that bag and dump it over here." Jake already had a pretty good idea what was in it.

"I wonder why they didn't take our guns and com units?" Lenny asked, after he had emptied the contents of the bag onto the ground.

"Think about it," Jake said, as he rose unsteadily from the chair, relieved to stretch his legs at last. "They were useless to our pirate. The PW-2s were made by AWDCOR and contain molecular IDs. They can be traced back to your RS team. The com units, of course, can only be used by their owners."

"Be sure not to activate the coms," RS-20 reminded everyone, as she retrieved hers from the pile.

"Why not?" Jake asked. "I was hoping to call for a taxi-bot."

"The ear-coms should have been destroyed when our ship crashed. If they suddenly started to work, our presence—and exact location—would be detected."

"Damn. I didn't even think of that. I must be more tired than I thought. We need to get out of here and find a place to rest."

"Hey, Lenny," RS-20 called out, "why don't you send some of your guys to the top of that hill for a look-see?"

"Good idea. Come on, men—we'll all go. It'll be good for you to get your butts moving."

RS-20, are you sure you can trust this guy?

Not entirely. But Lenny and I came to an understanding when we were on the ship. Among other things, he wants to be part of the action.

***

It didn't take too long for Lenny and his team to come back down the hill.

"There are a few rustic buildings in that direction. . . . a couple of hours away," Lenny announced, pointing to a trail leading to a nearby woods. "That path should take us there."

"Okay—let's get going then," Jake decided. "Forget the chair. The battery pack is depleted anyway." He was only too happy to be walking again and to leave that damn chair behind.

***

They were in luck. The buildings Lenny and his team had spotted from the top of the hill turned out to be a family-operated business, which included a café and a small motel. It had taken them four hours to reach their destination. It would have been easier to follow the rural highway they could hear in the distance, but they stuck with the trail through the woods to avoid attracting attention. Their pirate hadn't bothered to leave them any water or food rations. By the time they arrived at the café, they were all hungry, thirsty, and more than a little irritable.

"Let me do the talking," RS-20 said, smoothing down her hair, trying to make herself more presentable, as she went through the door first. The café didn't seem to have any cooling system, but a creaky, out-of-balance ceiling fan was a welcome relief.

When the lone waiter looked up at them from his place at the empty counter, he stared at them with his mouth hanging open for several seconds before he spoke.

"Hey, Mr. Jeepers," the waiter whispered to a yellow cat stretched out under a nearby table, "look at 'em: An older lady, a mean-looking bald guy, and five—no six—young dudes with guns." Jake was relieved to hear this guy could count to six.

"Our transport broke down," RS-20 interrupted the waiter's conversation with the cat. "We need to eat and find rooms for the night."

"Sure. No problem." The waiter raised his eyebrows at the cat and then pointed to a family table near the window. "I'll bring you some water and menus," he added, but he didn't get up from his place at the counter. "Those are real modern-looking pistols. We only have old-fashioned guns around here. I don't have nothin' like that in my gun collection."

Jake looked at RS-20 and sighed. "The water—the menus? If you could—"

"The wha—? Oh, sure." The waiter finally started moving. "Ma, we got us some customers!" he called out to the kitchen, as he started filling a tray of glasses with ice and water. While Ma peeked out from the kitchen, the cat got up from his place under the table and casually made his way over to Jake. A moment later, Mr. Jeepers was stretched out on the floor again, licking his paws and purring, waiting for something a little more substantial than a cold glass of water.

***

After they had finished eating, Jake set up a tab with his own credit account. He hoped it hadn't been closed yet. When the transaction went through without a glitch, the waiter asked them how many rooms they needed.

"One room for the lady and a large room with extra beds for us men." Jake looked at RS-20, who nodded her approval.

"It's been a long day, everyone. Let's get some sleep. We have a big day ahead of us tomorrow."

Chapter 23

Nobody said much when they sat together at the same table the next morning. They were all too busy wolfing down the home-cooked breakfast, which included delicious non-simulated eggs, bacon, sausage, donuts, and strong-brewed coffee. Ma had outdone herself today.

"I think we need to split up when we head into the city," Jake said, sipping his coffee. "RS-20, maybe you should go with Lenny and his team. I'll travel back on my own."

"Do you think that's really wise?" RS-20 asked, as she dipped a piece of toast into an egg yolk.

"I've got some things I need to take care of."

Don't try to contact your family yet, Jake. It might be dangerous for them—and you.

Jake nodded and then motioned for the waiter. "We're done here. Can you call us up a small taxi-bot and a compact shuttle bus?"

"Sure. But they'll probably take 'til noon to arrive."

"That's okay." Jake paused as a young couple and their two kids entered the café and wandered over to a table near them. "Would it be all right if we sit at that other big table in the corner? We need to discuss some things."

"Sit anywhere you like. I'll make sure nobody disturbs you." The waiter had apparently noticed Jake's generous tip when he settled the tab.

***

They had been traveling for several hours through the rugged hills that led to Welton when the shuttle bus driver announced they needed to exchange power packs at a refueling station. RS-20 was looking forward to the break. Lenny and his team weren't the best traveling companions. Their juvenile observations and jokes made her feel like she was in high school again. As the transport pulled into the station, she wondered where Jake was by now.

It was just starting to rain when she left Lenny and his team in the van and jumped out the door, eager to get inside the station. She could hear them snickering and then laughing as she slammed the door behind her. They probably thought she was hurrying to use the restroom, but she actually needed to send a private message to the head of the RS Department.

The public com screen inside the station accepted recipient-to-pay messages. She was relieved when her message was answered within a few seconds after she finished sending it.

Got it, Bill wrote back. *You're coming with an RS team. I'll tell the delivery door guards to escort you to my private office. As requested, I won't tell Michael Nash—or anyone else. Am glad you're safe. Looking forward to the meeting. Later, Bill.*

RS-20 smiled to herself, deleted the message, and looked around for the restrooms, just as Lenny and his team were entering the station, still snickering like a bunch of kids on a school outing.

Everyone was already back in the van when RS-20 finally got on board.

"What took you so long?" Lenny asked.

"I was busy," RS-20 said, frowning. "By the way, Lenny, I'm surprised your tat system isn't back on."

"Yeah, Tattyman, I miss seeing it," a team member behind them jibed.

"It's out of juice," he answered sadly. "The tat

runs on a small implanted power unit. I left the wireless recharger on the ship."

RS-20 leaned forward in her seat to give directions to the driver and to ask him a question.

"Hey, lady," Lenny said, as she settled back and fastened her safety harness. "Where are we headed to?"

"Home, boys. RS headquarters. Mr. Thurst wants to see us."

A moment later, she nudged Lenny with her elbow and pointed to a console next to the driver. "Lenny, the driver says it's okay if you use his universal charger."

Lenny laughed, lifted the lid to the console, and quickly activated the charger. Within a few seconds, the intricate web of tats on both his arms began blinking. Charging was underway.

***

Jake's taxi-bot made it to Ed's favorite bar without stopping anywhere. He was tempted to tell the taxi to make a detour to his own house as soon as they reached the outskirts of Welton, but he knew he couldn't risk that. It was very unlikely that Becky and the kids would be there anyway.

It didn't take him long to get what he needed at

Ed's favorite bar. Although Ed had made many enemies through his line of work, everyone who hung out at the bar had liked him. The bartender, a friendly young woman with silky black hair, even had a key card to Ed's condo, just as Jake had hoped.

As he walked along the busy street from the bar to Ed's place, Jake wondered if RS-20 had completed her meeting with the head of the RS Department. He would find out soon enough. She would be contacting him through Ed's com screen at his condo. If that didn't work, they would risk activating their ear-coms. It was such a shame that BIs didn't work at this distance.

Ed's place looked the same, although his private pad for delivery drones looked a bit worse for wear. Somebody had probably sent Ed another explosive package—someone that didn't know he was already dead.

Jake waved the card over the door handle, assuming it would work. AWDCOR was in a slack hiring period, and the condo would still be empty. As the door opened, it made a series of announcements, including *Please Check Your Food Supply and Your Com has 147 Unread*

Messages.

The four rooms of the condo looked exactly the same, but they seemed empty without Ed. No one had been here since he and his father had been killed. When Jake activated the wall screen, it came on with a newsfeed showing images of their recent ship crash. He was pleased to hear it was impossible to identify the occupants because of the catastrophic nature of the accident.

He wandered into the kitchen, activated the coffee machine, and sat down at the table, considering what he needed to do next. RS-20 should be messaging anytime. He hoped she was successful, and he would soon get Becky and the kids freed from Norb's control.

With his hot cup of coffee in one hand, he searched through Ed's closet and found one of his better suits that was to his liking. The hat and sunglasses gave him a VIP look. After he adjusted his tie, he looked around the condo for a spare PW-2 and found one in an umbrella stand near the front door. Unfortunately, it had a safety lock with a DNA imprint, so he wouldn't be able to use it.

He went back to the kitchen and poured himself another cup of coffee. There was nothing to do now but wait for RS-20's message.

Chapter 24

Bill Thurst sat in silence at his desk as he watched the recording that RS-20 had brought to him. When it showed the CADS drone opening fire on the children as they played tag in the schoolyard below, she saw him flinch, but he didn't speak for several more minutes. RS-20 could hear Lenny and his team growing restless as they stood near the door, fully armed, eager to carry out an order, but she didn't turn to look at them. She just watched Bill's face, feeling sorry for him. He appeared a little more tired than usual—and a little more gray. Being the head of the RS wasn't an easy job.

When Bill finally spoke, RS-20 could hear the tension in his voice as he tried to control his emotion. "I can't believe what I just saw. I knew we had problems with AWDCOR and Charles Milton, but I never suspected anything like this."

"I tried to warn you about Michael Nash."

He nodded at her as their eyes met, offering an unspoken apology. "What do you suggest we do now?" he asked. She knew if Lenny and his team weren't in the room, he would have said much more.

"Nash's mere dismissal won't be enough," RS-20 said.

"Agreed."

"And Jake Worthington needs our help. His boss, Norbert Goff, is in league with Nash."

"Hey," Lenny spoke up for the first time, "don't forget about us. My team and I have a score to settle with Nash and this Norbert guy."

"I'm not forgetting you, Lenny," RS-20 answered. "We have to find out where Nash keeps the controller to that drone."

"Let's pay Nash a visit right now," Bill said, standing up, ready to get everything resolved. "Lenny, I'm sure you can help Nash find that drone controller device in no time."

As they headed down the hall together to Nash's office, Bill turned to Lenny for a moment. "Please refrain from shooting him—at least for a while."

***

Nash looked up from his desk and gasped.

Lenny's PW-2 had him covered.

"But you're supposed to be dead," Nash said, without thinking.

"Stand up and walk away from the desk," Lenny ordered. "Right now, you SOB."

In spite of his shortcomings, RS-20 had to admit to herself that Lenny could be very useful at times. He knew how to handle situations like this. And she had to smile that his tat system was back online. Both arms were showing a person being disemboweled.

"W-wait—w-wait. I did it for the department," Nash was pleading, as he stepped away from his desk. "Hear me out. Bill, tell Lenny to stand down."

"Let's hear it, Nash. Keep him covered, Lenny," Bill said, as he drew closer to Nash.

"Norbert and I came up w-with an idea to develop a perfect w-weapon to handle rogue VIPs w-which w-would be invisible and leave no traces. Somebody at the AWDCOR factory screwed up and brought un-w-wanted attention to our CADS prototype—the Camouflaged Assassination Drone System. I had to make sure CADS was fully developed and ready for use. Bill, you must understand our need for such a w-w-weapon!"

Before Bill could respond, RS-20 spoke up, "Bill and I would like to know more about this CADS weapon. How do you control it?"

"Easy," Nash said, relaxing a little, smiling slightly. "I'll show you. I'll have to unlock my desk to retrieve the control unit."

"Not so fast," Lenny said, still pointing his PW-2 at him. "Put the key card on the desk, and Mr. Thurst will retrieve it."

Lenny's team had silently split into two groups and had moved to each side of Nash, ready to restrain him if necessary.

"This looks like a simple game pad controller with a small screen," Bill said, looking at it for a moment before he handed it over to RS-20. "Take it and see how it works. But be careful. We don't want any more accidents," he added, eyeing Nash. Bill's voice was still smooth and controlled, but RS-20 could tell he was doing everything in his power to keep from throttling Nash with his bare hands.

Chapter 25

Charles Milton was at home when his com screen alerted him that a priority text message had been received. His position as CEO of AWDCOR never allowed him a moment's rest.

Charlie, we need to talk right away. I'll be taking a heli-drone to the roof garden of AWDCOR headquarters. ETA in 23 minutes. Be sure to invite Norbert Goff. I'd like to have a little chat about CADS, okay? Thanks! Regards, Bill Thurst

Charles stared at the message on the screen. The head of the RS was being friendly. He quickly responded.

Bill, I'll be happy to meet with you. Norb is already at work. That man has been in the office a lot lately. Hope we can have a productive meeting. I'll order some drinks. Regards, Charlie

Charles touched the encrypt-and-send icon on the screen. A few seconds later, the icon signaled the message had been received and read.

***

Jake, it's ON. Get over to the parking lot across the street from Ed's. A heli-drone will be there to take you to AWDCOR headquarters.

Jake let out a sigh of relief when he read RS-20's message on Ed's com screen. He grabbed his hat and ear-com, secured the front door, and hurried across the street, dodging a few empty taxi-bots as he went. A 2-person heli-drone was already waiting for him.

When the door opened, he was surprised to find an older, silver-haired man that he had met once before sitting in one of the seats. It was Mr. Thurst, the head of the RS.

"Jake—good to see you again. Here—take this PW-10. It's already been set up by the RS team."

"Thanks, I suspect it might be useful." Jake checked to be sure the weapon was set to safe before he tucked it under his coat.

"Please fasten your flight harness," the drone reminded him, as the door slid shut. "We will lift off when it has been safely secured."

The flight to AWDCOR headquarters was swift, precise, and relatively smooth. Jake was glad the sun hadn't set yet. He liked to see where they were going as the drone flew a few hundred feet above the city traffic, weaving in and out of the taller skyscrapers to avoid hitting them.

When they landed on the rooftop drone pad at AWDCOR headquarters, Jake wasn't surprised to see five armed guards stationed near the CEO's garden gate entrance. As the heli-drone was thanking them for flying and wishing them a good night, Jake and Mr. Thurst ducked under the swirling blades and casually walked together toward the gate. When Mr. Thurst motioned to him, Jake adjusted his hat and coat to shield his face from direct view.

"Good afternoon, gentlemen," one of the guards said. "Mr. Milton is expecting you."

Across the rooftop garden, through the branches of the exotic plants and potted trees, they could see that Mr. Milton was already sitting at his regular table. Norb was seated across from him, his hands hovering over something on the table in front of him. It looked like a small drone with a clear plastic shell. As they headed in that direction, Jake and Mr. Thurst slowed their pace to hear exactly what they were saying.

"Norb, what's this?" Mr. Milton was asking rather loudly. "Is it a laser weapon of some sort? Is this a demo model of the CADS that Bill was talking about?"

"Yes," Norb answered enthusiastically, his attention focused entirely on the drone. "It's an ultraviolet laser with ionization blocking and a beam trace that's almost completely invisible. This is only a working model, of course, but it can still burn off an arm or leg." Norb sounded so proud of himself.

"But, Norb," they heard Mr. Milton say, "a weapon like this almost killed me—and didn't something like this kill Edward Shaw and his father? I thought you said no illegal weapons were being developed at Factory 309."

Norb started to reply but stopped when he finally noticed Jake and Mr. Thurst approaching their table.

"Michael Nash," Norb laughed. "You sure look different with that hat and those shades."

"I'm more different than you think," Jake answered, tossing his hat and sunglasses onto the table, almost hitting the small drone.

"Damn!" Norb said, grabbing the drone protectively. "Jake Worthington! We can never seem to kill you, can we?"

"Norbert—what's going on here?" Mr. Milton

asked, glancing nervously at Mr. Thurst. Talking about killing someone wasn't any way to impress the head of the RS Department.

Jake stepped closer to the table. "Listen, Norb: I want to know where my family is, and I want to know now. What have you done with them?" Although Jake could feel the PW-10 close to his side beneath his coat, he made no effort to reach for it.

"Oh," Norb waved his hand dismissively, "don't get your shorts twisted into such a knot. They're in the basement—alive and well. I don't waste anything that can be sold for profit."

"Norb!" Mr. Milton scolded, jumping up from his place at the table.

"Sit down, Mr. Milton," Norb said, still seated calmly at the table with the drone. "I want to demonstrate exactly how this neat little CADS unit works." He smiled as he retrieved a handheld controller from his pocket and released the drone into the air. It hovered for a moment above the table before it turned to Jake and aimed its tiny weapon at him. "It's time to get rid of you once and for all, Jake Worthington."

"No!" Mr. Milton yelled, jumping to his feet

again, swiping his hand toward the drone, trying to swat it from the air. He missed. The drone's automatic evasive maneuvering was much too fast for him, but the movement was enough for it to miss its target. Jake could feel the heat from the weapon's beam as it went past his head. A moment later, a tree on the other side of the rooftop garden fell over, its trunk burned and severed.

Jake and Mr. Thurst pulled out their PW-10s, just as Mr. Milton swiped at the drone again. This time the drone turned toward the CEO and found its target. Mr. Milton screamed in pain and slumped to the floor, clutching his shoulder. The sleeve of his coat was smoldering, exposing his burned flesh to the air.

Mr. Thurst tried to wrench the controller from Norb's hand while Jake fired his weapon directly at Norb. Unfortunately, he missed.

When the projectile hit him in the chest, Mr. Thurst frowned at Jake for a moment and then fell limp across the table, barely missing Norb as he was dodging for cover with the controller still in his hand. The drone turned and fired. Jake felt the searing heat from the blast and smelled his hair and flesh burning, but he didn't have time to check to see if he still had both of his ears.

He began running backwards, firing at Norb as he went. He could see the guards scurrying across the rooftop garden with their weapons drawn, dodging in and out of the potted trees. Jake kept running backwards, firing at Norb, only stopping when he suddenly smashed straight into the decorative lattice at the edge of the building. For one long moment, he thought the lattice was going to hold him, but a second later, he found himself dropping his PW-10, grabbing for the metal eave, and dangling three stories above the busy street below. As he hung there, trying to maintain his grip, he noticed how cool and pleasant the evening air seemed to be and how long it seemed to take for his PW-10 to fall to the ground, only to be hit by a bus-bot—and then another. At that moment, he glanced up and saw Norb's drone coming over the edge of the roof. He could already feel the fabric on his suit's collar starting to melt.

"It's okay," he heard Norb saying to the guards on the rooftop. "I can take care of him from here—but stand by."

The small CADS drone was now hovering to one side of Jake, its laser pointed at his head.

"So long, Jake," Norb said, smiling down at

him from the edge of the roof. "Too bad your family can't see this. Hey—I know," he said with the smile of a true psychopath, "—I'll make a recording for them."

As Norb fumbled for his ear-com, Jake could see Lenny and his team taking positions at the delivery entrance in the rear of the rooftop garden.

Jake, where are you?

RS-20! Thank God! I'm hanging from the roof near the northwest corner of the building! Norb is going to burn off my head in a second!

Jake, close your eyes! I'm going to fire the CADS drone!

No! The drone's right next to my head!

Not that drone! Michael Nash's drone is hovering above Norb. Close your eyes!

Jake did as he was told. He could hear a fire-fight erupting between the AWDCOR guards and Lenny's team, just as RS-20 warned him once more that she was firing the invisible CADS drone that was directly above Norb. A second later, when Jake opened his eyes again, Norb was gone. There was nothing left of him but a sizzling liquid dripping down the side of the building and a cloud of blue-colored smoke rising above the rooftop garden. The small drone hovering in the air at

Jake's side fell to the street below and then bounced onto the sidewalk, where it landed intact.

Jake repositioned his grip on the metal eave, kicked his feet in the air, and managed to pull himself up to peer over the edge of the rooftop. Mr. Thurst was still slumped across the table. Mr. Milton was lying on the floor nearby, barely conscious.

"Watch out!" Jake shouted, trying to warn one of Lenny's men that an AWDCOR guard was coming up from behind him.

He was too late. The young RS agent had been distracted by the sizzling liquid and blue smoke which Norb had left behind. When the guard fired, Lenny's teammate fell flat to the floor, his eyes still open, staring at the night sky. Jake lost his grip on the metal eave and slipped down the side of the building again. It was just as well. An all-out firefight was taking place on the rooftop now.

In less than a minute, the sounds of PW weapons suddenly stopped. Jake managed to work himself back up to the top of the building and peered over the edge of the rooftop garden once more. Broken lattice and toppled trees blocked most of his view. All he could see was Lenny, with his weapon drawn, walking straight toward him.

"Uh, Jake," he said, "take my hand. Let's get you back on the roof." As Lenny pulled him up, he added, "I'm guessing you shot Mr. Thurst. Well, it could have been worse. Those AWDCOR SOBs had their PW-2s set to kill. I lost one guy. I'm sorely tempted to toss all of them off the roof."

"Thanks, Lenny. I'm sorry about your teammate."

Lenny's tats on his right arm flashed a polite salute before he suddenly turned and yelled, "Hey, team! Watch that staircase! I'm sure more guards are headed up that way!"

Jake wiped his hands on his coat. Both of them were bleeding from his tight grip on the metal gutter. His left ear hurt like hell. He looked around. What a mess. Bill Thurst was crumpled on the table. RS-20 was standing next to him, with a weapon in one hand and a controller in the other. She looked up at Jake and nodded. Bill was going to be all right. Mr. Milton was still writhing and moaning in pain under the table. One of Lenny's team members was dead on the floor. The five AWDCOR guards were lying scattered across the rooftop garden. They were all twitching, but at least they were alive. The PW projectiles had left dozens of pock mocks across the garden's tiled floor. They had worked as designed, releasing acid and dissolving every hard surface they encountered.

"Jake," RS-20 said, as he approached her and Mr. Thurst. "The medics are on their way. Are you all right? It looks like you'll need some work on that ear." She paused to verify that the CADS drone was leaving the area, and its safety logic was engaged.

Without warning, another firefight started to break out near the main stairwell door. RS-20 provided covering fire as she and Jake ducked behind a large planter near Mr. Milton.

"Jake, we're running low on ammo!" Lenny yelled, sliding his last ammo clip into place.

Mr. Milton, who was still whimpering from his burns, motioned for Jake to come to his side under the table. He left RS-20 behind the planter and crawled over to the CEO.

"Jake, I trusted Norb like a son. I'm sorry for all of this. Drop by my office as soon as I'm better. We have some things to discuss. I'm getting too old to run this company."

"Mr. Milton!" Jake interjected, as a projectile

barely missed them and then hit the floor right next to RS-20. "We have to stop this fight before more people are killed!"

Mr. Milton tried to reach for the com unit that he kept in his vest, but he was too weak. "Jake, in my vest pocket. . . . my com unit. . . . hit the green button 3 times."

Jake found the com device and quickly punched the green button 3 times.

"AWDCOR guards," the PA system suddenly announced. "Stand down. Mr. Milton has given the all-clear signal." The sounds of the firefight became more sporadic and then stopped completely as the message repeated itself over and over again for the next minute.

"Thanks, Mr. Milton," Jake said. "I look forward to meeting with you later."

Mr. Milton nodded, closed his eyes, and lost consciousness completely. Jake wasn't sure he knew that Norb had been killed.

Several medical heli-drones were landing on the rooftop. RS-20 emerged from her position behind the potted plant and made her way toward Bill Thurst, but she kept glancing around her with her weapon drawn, ready for more trouble.

"Jake, I think it's over. Wait a few minutes and

go to the basement. Take some of Lenny's team with you, just in case somebody didn't get the stand-down order."

Four medics began working on Mr. Thurst and Mr. Milton. A fifth medic came over to Jake and applied first aid ointment and bandages to his ear.

A few minutes later, Jake finally headed down to the basement with several members of Lenny's team to find his family.

Chapter 26

Jake and Becky were awakened in their bed by the cook-bot chiming from the kitchen that breakfast was being prepared. They could hear that Lucy and Jacob were already up, playing a virtual reality game in the living room. Jake had told them last night they could skip school for a few days. They were taking full advantage of their holiday.

Jake had been able to get some sleep, in spite of the discomfort from his ear, but he couldn't stop himself from getting up several times during the night to check in on the kids. It seemed strange to go down the empty hall without stepping over Fluffy. He still couldn't believe their sweet old dog wouldn't be coming home.

The cook-bot chimed again from the kitchen.

"I'd better go," Becky said, sitting up to feel for her house slippers on the floor. Sometimes the cook-bot got confused and fried the waffles and boiled the bacon.

"Kids, get dressed and cleaned up for breakfast!" Becky called. "I expect everyone at the table in 10 minutes. Jake," she added with a quick pat on his leg, "let's get moving!"

When Jake and the kids finally shuffled into the kitchen, Becky gave them all a kiss on the cheek. "Jake, it's okay with me if you start shaving again," she whispered in his ear.

Jake smiled at her and then noticed all the filled dishes that the kitchen-bot was bringing to the table. "There's enough food here to feed ten people."

"We're starving," Becky answered enthusiastically. "We had nothing but outdated ration packs for a week. The kids and I hardly ate at all."

Jake nodded as Jacob and Lucy dug into their eggs and waffles. "I could eat a little more myself," he said, reaching for another waffle.

"Dad," Jacob asked, "when are you going to tell us what happened?"

"I hated Norb!" Lucy said suddenly, dropping her fork into the middle of her plate. "He was a horrible, mean man. I'm glad Fluffy bit him. I wish he had bit him a million times." She pushed her plate away. "Daddy," she said with a trembling lower lip, "Norb told a guard to shoot Fluffy."

Jake reached over and patted the back of her

hand. "I know, baby. . . . Norb won't be hurting anyone anymore."

At that moment, the kitchen com screen announced someone was approaching the front door. The porch sensors indicated that the person was unarmed and wasn't carrying explosives or bio-hazardous materials. Jake smiled when he saw who was coming.

"That's a surprise. Becky, it's the RS-20 agent I was telling you about."

"Good. I'll set another place at the table."

Jake unlocked the door and held it open. "You're just in time for breakfast! Come in and meet Becky and the kids."

"Hello, Jake—wait a second. What's that?" she asked, turning to point to the sky above the house across the street. "Is that a drone?"

Jake reached to retrieve a PW-2 from the DNA lockbox near the front door. He stopped when he saw that it was only a small delivery drone. From its metal hook a puppy was dangling in the air, looking around at the world below it with wide, unblinking eyes. Jake laughed. The drone was carrying the puppy by the nape of its neck as gently as a mother dog.

"I was hoping it would arrive on time," RS-20

said, as she reached up to release the puppy and handed it to Jake. It wagged its tail, licked his hand, and quickly snuggled close to his chest.

"Now let's go in and meet your family," RS-20 said with a smile. "It's a small hairless breed," she added. "Lenny helped me pick him out."

The puppy wasn't only hairless—he also had a tat system on his bare skin, just like Lenny's. When they entered the kitchen, it suddenly turned on, displaying a food bowl and then a patch of green lawn.

As soon as the kids saw the puppy, they jumped up from the table, squealing with delight.

"You'd better take him outside, and then we'll find him some food," Becky laughed.

After they ran outside with the puppy held tight in Lucy's arms, Jake turned to his wife. "Becky, I'd like to formally introduce you to the agent who saved my life, but I just realized I don't know her name."

"It's good to meet you, Becky," RS-20 said, extending her hand. "Your husband didn't need that much saving. My name is Jeanette Graham, but my friends call me Jean. RS-20 is perfectly fine too. Actually, I hear that more than anything."

"RS-20, is Bill Thurst still improving? And Michael Nash—where's he at now?" Jake asked.

"Bill's out of the hospital. . . . I'm on his personal staff now, in charge of RS internal affairs. Lenny and his team have received promotions and will be reporting directly to me. Nash is in confinement awaiting transfer to an off-planet prison. He's been charged with the murders of your partner and his father, plus the attempted murder of Mr. Milton. Bill hasn't decided what kind of transfer Nash will be given. Lenny really wants to help make it an extra-special trip to prison, but we'll see about that."

"What about the CADS drones?"

"Both of the CADS drones have been taken to a secure location." RS-20 held up her hand before he could protest. "I know—I know—you don't need to tell me, Jake. But I can assure you they'll be safely stored in a secret government warehouse. Bill said you never know when they might turn out to be useful someday. We think there may be more around. We'll be looking for them at AWDCOR. Bill isn't happy with the CEO. We're going to have to talk about this pretty soon. . . . By the way, Bill said not to worry about you shooting him. It seems to be your trademark."

"It sounds like you two need to discuss some business. I'll go join the kids outside," Becky said, getting up from the table.

"Wait, honey. You need to hear this," Jake told her. "RS-20, I instructed Factory 309 to destroy all the CADS drones and the design data files. Building C-3 is now producing children's playground toys."

"Jake, can you actually do that?" RS-20 asked. "I mean, doesn't it take a CEO to authorize something like that?"

"Yeah, well, Mr. Milton decided he really had to retire off-planet. The new CEO can do anything he likes," Jake added, pointing to a diamond-studded gold tag behind his ear.

Both Becky and RS-20 gasped.

"I wondered what that was," Becky finally said. "I thought it had something to do with your ear surgery." Her voice had grown quiet. She was probably realizing how much their lives were about to change.

"There are going to be a lot of changes at AWDCOR," Jake said seriously. "I'm promoting some GAPs I met on Barros. They'll be running Factory 309 after I talk the local police into letting them out of jail."

The back door sprung open as the kids came running back in. Lucy was still holding the puppy tight in her arms.

"We're going to name him Killer," Jacob announced with a big grin.

"Killer?" Becky said, raising her eyebrows in disapproval.

Killer's tat system suddenly activated and displayed a bouquet of flowers in a variety of pastel colors. They all laughed.

"Killer sounds perfect," Jake said, putting his arm around Becky and motioning the kids and the puppy to come closer. He reached down to pat the puppy on his smooth, warm head.

"Welcome to the family, Killer," he said, winking at Becky and then smiling at RS-20. "Welcome to the family."

111915